guitar
highway
rose

guitar highway rose

brigid lowry

Excerpts on pages 22, 52, 62, 97 are from *Living with teenagers,* a publication produced by Family and Children's Services. The department provides services to support families in Western Australia.

The jokes on page 18 are from *Wallflowers: A Collection of Australian Graffiti,* ed. Bruce Ridley, Ridley Books, Melbourne, 1981.

www.stmartins.com

Library of Congress Cataloging-in-Publication Data

Lowry, Brigid.
Guitar highway Rose / Brigid Lowry.—1st St. Martin's Griffin ed.
p. cm.
First published in Australia by Allen & Unwin Pty Ltd.
Summary: Two fifteen-year-olds, Rosie and Asher, upset over the various unhappy circumstances of their lives in the Australian city of Perth, decide to run away.
ISBN 0-312-34296-9
EAN 978-0-312-34296-8
[1. Coming of age—Fiction. 2. Parent and teenager—Fiction. 3. Runaways—Fiction. 4. Australia—Fiction.] I. Title.

PZ7.L96725Gu 2005
[Fic]—dc22 2005046457

First published in Australia by Allen & Unwin Pty Ltd.
First published in the United States by Holiday House, Inc.

First St. Martin's Griffin Edition: July 2005

10 9 8 7 6 5 4 3 2 1

For Sam, who inspired Asher,

and for Paul, who keeps telling me I'm great.

My name is Rosie Moon. My star sign is Aries. I come from a long line of women who have flower names. I am nearly sixteen. I live near the sea. I like reading, roses, swimming, late nights, chocolate, clouds. I'm hungry for a juicy life. I lean out the window at night and I can taste it out there, just waiting for me.

guitar
highway
rose

ROSIE/SATURDAY MORNING

I can't get started. Our new English teacher, Mr Epanomitis, says we have to write a self portrait set in the past, the present or the future, five hundred words, make it creative and interesting, due in on Monday. Sounds easy. Isn't.

How about this . . .

My name is Rosie Moon. I have a middle name as well but I won't tell you what it is because I hate it. I am fifteen and desperate. My mother won't let me get a nose-ring. She thinks they are unsightly and what if I want to be a lawyer one day? Who cares what she thinks? She's becoming a boring old person who says no to everything. She is just so neurotic these days. Also I have tinea on my foot and my brother won't get off the computer. My parents are probably going to split up and I almost wish they would. I'm sick of hearing them fighting late at night or talking to each other in frosty, polite voices as if Harry and I were so dumb we would be fooled by that. It is incredibly hot, my foot itches like mad, my room could do with a blitz but I can't be bothered and I'm not allowed to go to the beach until I've done my homework. Whoop de doo . . .

No way I can hand that in, even though Mr E seems like an okay person. He has a ponytail and wears jeans and a blue denim shirt. Better than last year's boring old Mrs 'Quiet Class' Radisson. Hard to have been worse though. Mrs R was the pits. This is getting me nowhere fast. Start again.

I am Rosie Moon. I am fifteen years old and I live in an old house near the sea with my parents, my brother Harry and our cat, Beethoven. My father's name is Robert and my mother's name is Lily. All the women in our family are given flower names. My grandmother is Violet, my aunt is Daphne and my cousins are Heather and Fleur. It's stupid, I reckon. Soon they'll run out of flower names. What am I supposed to call my kids if I have them, Gladioli and Carnation? The boys get called sensible things like Ned and Harry, not Burdock or anything ridiculous. They should have called Harry 'Thistle' because he is a thorn in my side and a pain in the butt. Eight is a difficult age, my mother says, but she said that about seven as well. I do love Harry and all but sometimes he drives me bananas. He doesn't close his mouth when he chews his food and he never . . .

Far out, I'm way off beam here. This is supposed to be a self portrait, not a whinge about my younger brother. Third time lucky. Even if it's putrid I'm going to hand it in. Beach and blue waves here I come.

SELF PORTRAIT

My name is Rosie E Moon. I am fifteen years old. My star sign is Aries on the cusp with Pisces, which is why I am a creative warrior-woman from Mars who loves to swim. I live in a house in

Swanbourne with my parents, Robert and Lily, my brother Harry, and a cat named Beethoven. My best friend is called Pippa and she has blue hair. She comes from New Zealand and is part Maori. Her parents, Vera and Joseph, are totally cool. She *is allowed a nose-ring, well, it's a little red glass stud actually.*

♥ **WHAT I LIKE:** roses, beach, music, sleeping in, old hippie clothes, chocolate anything, late nights, reading, clouds.

☠ **WHAT I DON'T LIKE:** raisins in curry, cold coffee, being told what to wear, dog-shit on my shoe, adults who talk about what a mess the world is in and do nothing about it, runny eggs.

PIP AND ROSIE AT THE BEACH

Shall we go in again? asks Pip.

Nah, let's just rest for a while. Can I wear your shirt? I'm getting sunburnt. Where did you get it?

Yeah, sure. It used to be Mum's. Look at my knees, they're so podgy.

They are not. Don't be mad.

Are so, look at them. Anyhow, what are you doing tonight?

Nothing. My parents want a quiet night. Would you be allowed to come over?

Nah, we're going to this big party, my uncle's birthday. With a live band and a big feast and everything.

Cool. Look at that kid over there, the one with the striped jacket on.

Yeah, never seen him before. Wonder why he's wearing a jacket at the beach. He must be so hot.

Yeah. Cool looking, though.

Look at his hair . . . Marley dreads.

Mmm, wicked. Wonder who he is?

Yeah, never seen him before.

ROSIE'S BEDROOM:

Double bed with blue-and-white Balinese bedspread. Battered panda bear named Hartley. Blue satin pillow. Gilded mirror shaped like a sun. Clothes, assorted: frilly, drifty, floaty, baggy, tatty. Squashy old armchair draped with a white lace tablecloth. Shoes, three pairs: black Docs, grubby sneakers, red sandals. Books. Dragon ornament. Collection of things made of blue and red glass. Photo of Rosie and Pip coming out of the sea, festooned with seaweed. Desk with huge amount of stuff on it, including address book with roses on cover, coloured pencils, Cherry Ripe wrapper, one loose tampon, one Gary Larson book, small kaleidoscope, plastic pineapple, sunscreen, mascara, glitter, Mickey Mouse clock.

ROSIE/SATURDAY NIGHT

Nothing to do. Mum and Dad are watching 'The Bill' and Harry is playing 'Doom III' on the computer. I hate 'The Bill'. It's the same every week and depressing. The beach was fun, though. Pip met me there and we swam for ages and just lazed round.

I've even tidied my room a bit to stop Mum carrying on endlessly about it. She just nags and nags. It's my room and I don't see why she can't accept that. Anyway, I thought I'd lost my sunglasses at school but I found them under the bed, which is somewhat helpful.

Purple silk kimono. Hot summer night. White roses from the garden in a red glass vase. Looking out the window down to the sea. Wish I could go out. Do something. Be someone. Be someone else. Restless and lonely and bored. Just re-read my homework and I hate it. Me in the present isn't very interesting. Also it is way too short, nowhere near five hundred words. Maybe the future? *Rose Starflower lives on Venus. For breakfast she ingests an electron rainbow pill* . . . how dumb. No one knows what the future will be like or even if humans will survive. I think I'll write an imaginary portrait set in the past, in the Rocks area of Sydney, where we went on holiday last year. I'll hand that in along with the one that's really about me. Mr Epanomitis said we could be creative. Who might I have been if I wasn't me?

OLD TIME ROSE

My name is Rose and I was born on the 17th of March, 1934. I am an autumn child, one of the seven children of Patrick and Ruby Murphy, Irish immigrants who run a small grocery shop in the docks area of Sydney. My father planted us, my mother named us after flowers, and then we were left to fend for ourselves. My sisters are called Lily and Violet. They are much older than me and they work in the shop, weighing out rice and tea and broken biscuits and packing them in paper bags. My baby brother sleeps in a drawer, wrapped in a little blanket of patchwork satin. Rory and Young Pat play marbles and rowdy ball games in the street and come home ravenous and covered in mud. At night William, my eldest brother, plays jigs and lovesongs on his fiddle as we all sit by the fire, my mother knitting socks and my father scratching his head over bills for sacks of rice and wheels of cheese. I have long red hair which I wear in a thick plait and wash once a week in the tin bathtub. My father says I am the fairest rose of Ireland, but really I am covered in freckles and taller and thinner than any girl in our street. I do not like to be called Broomstick, and my favourite foods are dumpling stew and hot potatoes baked in the coals.

CONTENTS OF ASHER'S POCKETS:

1 large men's handkerchief with green stripe, dirty.

1 Mars bar wrapper, very scrunched.

1 packet of matches advertising the Universal wine bar, found on street.

1 packet of cigarette papers.

Balinese wallet made of rainbow batik, containing a keycard, a photograph of three people, $2.20, a pencil stub and a Chinese *I Ching* coin with a hole in it.

ASHER/MONDAY MORNING

what oh god mum in her fuzzy dressing gown with her hair all sticking up what get up love it's seven o'clock that worried voice oh shit first day of new school have to be there at eight thirty wish i could just sleep all day roll over in the warmth and drift off again i was dreaming something i was climbing rocks climbing way up high and a hawk on my shoulder yeah yeah mum I'm up already into the shower which shampoo am I supposed to use this one will do for normal hair why does everything have to be normal i want one for strange hair rinse it out don't worry about conditioner damn no towel mum where's a towel where's my jeans yesterday's socks under the bed that'll do need new shoelaces on my docs yes mum I'm coming black t-shirt and i am definitely going to wear my jacket i love my jacket really cool op shop only three bucks covers up my skinny arms makes me look stylish as hell yes mum here i am yes i am going to wear it because i want to that's why no i won't be too hot she's definitely in anxious mode today mmm yum wake me up coffee thanks mum plenty of brown sugar big slosh of soyamilk on my cereal oops spilled it never mind stupid cardboard packets impossible to pour from bad design maybe i could design new brilliantly pouring packet get rich oh shit eight o'clock do teeth i *am* wearing it okay who cares about stupid dress code tight guts no way do i want to face this new school those eyes everyone staring at me not knowing anyone trying to find my way around i wish today was over come home watch tv do my own thing yes mum I've got my lunch yes mum yes I've got my bag wish i was back at the bay wish i was anywhere but here . . .

DRESS CODE/BIRCH STREET HIGH

'Our school colours are blue, red and white. Neat and tidy

garments in all of these colours are to be worn by all students. Blazers with the school crest are available from the office. Black, patterned or clothing with logos are not permitted. Jewellery should not be worn. Students not adhering to the rules will be given a dress pass. Three dress passes mean detention. All students are asked to respect the dress code.'

FAVOURITE QUIPS OF THE RICH AND FAMOUS

ROSIE: In the beginning God created Heaven and Earth. Then she dozed off and created Perth.

ROSIE'S FATHER: Margaret River Cabernet Sauvignon kills ninety-nine per cent of household germs.

ROSIE'S MOTHER: Is there a heaven and does it take Bankcard?

PIP: Save the earwig!

HARRY: Do your underpants have holes in them? No, well then, how do you get your legs in?

MR EPANOMITIS: Man is an absurd, helpless mortal creature lost in a hostile and meaningless universe. Thank goodness we've still got Channel Seven.

ASHER'S MOTHER: Choose a slow lingering death. Get married.

ASHER: Be aloof. Your country needs loofs.

ROSIE/MONDAY NIGHT

Guess what happened today? A new kid started at our school, the same boy that Pip and I saw at the beach on Saturday. We noticed him because he had this black-and-white striped jacket on and he looked neat, except he must have been boiling hot. His name is Asher. He comes from Byron Bay, which Pip says is a hippie area in New South Wales. He had the groovy jacket on today, and a black t-shirt. I guess they won't give him a dress pass until he has settled in. He sat at the back and didn't say much. We were doing iambic pentameter so who can blame him?

I like him. He looks kind of sad and intelligent. I haven't told anyone this, not even Pip, but just when the siren went at the end of class I was sort of sneaking a look at him and he winked at me. I felt pretty stunned but I winked back. At least I hope it looked like a wink. I'm not that good at winking and it might have just come across like a squashed-up goofy face. Anyhow, Asher is the most interesting thing that has happened in my life lately. Next time I see him I'm going to talk to him, if I can think of what to say. I might tell Pip after all and see what she suggests. She's not at all shy, Pip isn't. Mum says she could talk the leg off a chair. Harry says she could sure organise a root in a brothel. Mum goes absolutely spare when he says it. I don't know where he got it from, heard Dad say it probably and then got it back to front. Funny old Harry. Anyway, I handed in my self-portrait thing to Mr E. Hope I get it back soon. Mrs Radisson used to take for ever to mark things. Even the tinea on my foot is getting better. Life is looking up.

ASHER'S AFTER SCHOOL SNACK:
rice cakes with peanut butter and honey cup of coffee two sugars bowl of stewed apple one last rice cake

ASHER/SURVIVOR OF DAY ONE AT BIRCH STREET HIGH

where's mum thought she'd be home by now well i did it not that bad i suppose not that good though either what a boring straight school that girl was strange though staring at me in english shouldn't have winked at her didn't really mean to now she'll think i like her didn't like the vibes at birch street all those awful sirens blaring and all those look-alike people very tedious not like byron bay wish i was back there i wish no good wishing is it i wonder what viv and sam and jesse are doing wonder if jesse will write to me she said she would but no use really so far away her purple lace skirt her red dreads her mad laugh it was special it was her and me and viv and sam it was fish and chips on the beach and late into the night it was the best and now it's gone this flat is horrible it smells putrid maybe there's a gas leak better have a look that sounds like mum man am i hungry

WHAT ASHER WISHES HE COULD FORGET

The day his parents finally called it quits.

SHORT DESCRIPTION OF THE BEACH ON WHICH LILY IS ABOUT TO WALK

The sky is blue, catch-your-breath blue, and the frilled edge of the Indian Ocean is dancing in waves of vivid turquoise and murky green. The ice-white sand is decorated with generous dollops of fresh and dried dog-poop and garlands of seaweed, dimpled necklaces of sea-beads ready to pop. Out on the horizon a container ship sits squat and solid, waiting to come into port, carrying shoes from China, perhaps, or frozen fish, or expensive antiques. Two tanned men in tight fluoro shorts jog effortlessly past. A mother helps her fat-legged toddler make a sandcastle with a red bucket and spade, and a freckled boy throws a tennis ball. The fat guy who is always there is doing his unique blubbery version of star jumps. There's a white beach umbrella and a lost thong and four dogs: a dalmatian, a fluffy thing, a Jack Russell terrier and a mutt with a mean-looking head. The fragrance is salty sea-breeze with a dash of coconut suntan oil.

LILY WALKING ON THE BEACH

Why doesn't that container ship sink? wonders Lily, remembering the science experiments she did in primary school, putting things in water, seeing what sank and what floated. Corks floated and heavy things sank, she remembers, so how come a heavy container ship floats? Also, how come planes stay in the air when tennis balls come straight down again? With planes it must be to do with energy and petrol, but with those huge heavy ships it's something to do with dispersed mass, whatever that is . . . I should have done physics so I understood that sort of thing properly, thinks Lily.

She is having a bad hair, bad luck day; her thighs feel fat and the morning's fighting at the breakfast table is still with her in the form of tight neck muscles and a head full of anxious thoughts. I handle it all wrong, Lily agonises. I shouldn't have yelled at Harry for spilling his muesli all over the floor. It's not as if he meant to, I guess. It's just that the biodynamic stuff is so expensive and he is *such* a scatterbrain. I should have given Robert a friendly goodbye when he left for work but he seemed so cold, why should I be the one to make all the effort? And then there's Rosie. Things are going from bad to worse with me and Rosie. What's happening to us? We disagree about everything these days. Last year we were happy and close and now I can't get near her. And what about this dreadful nose-ring business? There's no way I'm letting her get one of those. They look absolutely terrible. She'd soon regret it. What if she wants to be a lawyer or something. Yet she wants it so badly. Oh, hell, is that the time? I'm going to be late for the dentist.

From LIVING WITH TEENAGERS

'As the teenager moves towards being an independent adult it is necessary for parents to scale down their attempts to control the child — gradually and appropriately. Parents should give their teenager the opportunity to make his/her own choices, decisions and mistakes, so that he/she can develop independence and self-responsibility.'

MEET ROBERT

At forty-four his favourite cartoonist is Leunig. At forty-four he has his first white hairs and pulls them out when no one is looking. At forty-four he jokes that old is twenty years older than he is now. At forty-four he thinks he might join a men's group to talk about his feelings but he has difficulty with feelings, although he is good at thoughts. At forty-four he thinks it would be goofy to wear t-shirts with silly phrases on them but he wants to just the same. At forty-four he wishes he had gone to film school instead of becoming a lawyer. At forty-four he sits in coffee bars and wonders how much cholesterol is in a blueberry danish and whether the waitress tells *her* husband she's too tired to make love most nights. At forty-four he still doesn't give a toss about superannuation, mortgage rates and the consumer price index. At forty-four he'd rather be sailing.

HARRY'S BEDROOM:

A bed shaped like a red car. Looney Toons curtains. Two hand-held computer games, one functional, one not. Tin of condensed milk and spoon hidden under the bed. Four *Mad* comics. Wet boardshorts hanging out the window. Soggy towel on floor. Uneaten school lunch tucked neatly under pile of clean underwear in top drawer. Nike and Mambo t-shirts along with Target cheapo t-shirts. Huge amount of Lego, scattered high and low. A hopelessly knotted slinky. Two goldfish in a tank: Jerry and Arnie. Various rocks, shells, birds' eggs and birds' nests. Moneybox shaped like radio. Radio shaped like Coke can. Actual Coke can, empty. Socks, random selection. Half-done project about dinosaurs.

HARRY SAYS:

My sister Rosie is tall and she looks like a gypsy because she has long dark curls and she wears colourful skirts and stuff. I like it when she plays on the computer with me and also when she looks out for me if Mum is in a bad mood. Sometimes she goes in her room and won't come out and Mum gets really poopy with her and they scream at each other. I hate that. A brother who had a CD ROM would have been good but Rosie is pretty cool. She thinks Beethoven is her cat but he isn't. He is half mine.

HOROSCOPE FOR ARIES/TUESDAY

Neptune is about to enter Aries, indicating mystery and illusion. Events are not what they seem. You can expect to find this a time of challenge and confusion.

ON TUESDAY MORNING PIP AND ROSIE WALK TO SCHOOL

Hey, Rosie, is your Mum in a shit or something?

Yeah, as usual. How did you guess?

She just seemed weird, when she was saying goodbye to us. Like she was trying to smile but feeling gruesome.

Yeah, well, gruesome is a good word for it. We had this mega fight at brekkie. Harry was goofing off and spilt his cereal and milk everywhere and Mum just lost it and yelled and carried on. She bit my head off when I said he didn't mean to and then raved on about me not brushing my hair. Brushing my hair if you don't mind . . . she treats me like I'm about four or something. She's like it all the time lately.

Yeah, parents, I dunno. Actually mine slept in this morning so I had the kitchen all to myself. Heaps of butter on my toast, heaps of sugar in my coffee, radio playing really loud, no one to say no. Good, hey?

Yeah. It's so hot already. What have you got first?

Health. Then Maths. Whoop dee doo. What have you got?

Double English. Hey, Pip.

What?

Nothing.

What do you mean, nothing?

Oh, don't worry about it.

Rosie. Tell me.

It's nothing, Pip. Well, not really anything. It's just that boy. The one we saw on the beach. Asher. Remember, I told you yesterday how he's in my English class?

Yeah, I know. The guy with dreads and a stripey jacket. So?

Well, he winked at me. That's all. In class. And I winked back, well, I tried to, except I think it came out all squashy.

Rosie! Why didn't you tell me?

I am telling you. Anyway, it's nothing.

It is so something. I mean, do you like him or what?

I don't know, Pip. I don't even know him. I guess I'd like to get to know him and . . . that's what I was wondering. Should I go and talk to him?

Yeah, why not? I would. I mean he must like you or he wouldn't have winked at you, would he?

Yeah, maybe. I don't know.

Go on, girl. It won't hurt.

Mmmm. Gee, it's hot. Let's go to the beach after school.

You're on, babe. Oh, shit. Let's run. There goes the siren.

WHAT ASHER WORE TO SCHOOL/ TUESDAY:

Green Doc Martens, size ten, scuffed, one complete shoelace, one not-all-there shoelace. Baggy dark-blue men's work trousers with ragged cuffs and two floral patches on bum. Short-sleeved rayon shirt with strange orange-and-brown pattern, circa 1964.

WHAT MRS HYDE, THE HOMEROOM TEACHER, HAD TO SAY

So, everyone, please make sure you bring your signed homework books each day without fail — no excuses tomorrow, please. And, because it is early in the term, I urge you all to set a good example for the Year Eight students by observing our dress code. It's so important they understand that we are tidy, well-groomed people at Birch Street. That will be all for now. Oh, and don't forget the fundraising raffle. Bring your money as soon as possible everyone. Jeremy, be quiet please. Off you go now, class, there's the siren. Ah, can I see you a moment, please. Yes, you. Ah, Asher, isn't it? Mmm. Asher, about your clothing. I didn't like to mention anything yesterday as it was your first day but I'm afraid it can't go any further than this. Mr McKenna assures me that you were given a copy of our dress code and I'd like to see you wearing some nice tidy clothing from now on. And as for that hairstyle, it could be a lot tidier, couldn't it, dear? Now, our school colours are red, white and blue. There's a second-hand uniform shop near the library that is open at lunchtime, you can tell your mother. Do you understand me?

Yes.

Well, off you go then, Asher.

ASHER/TUESDAY 9.15am

stupid old cow in your drab little suit understand you yeah sure i understand you but agree with you hell no i'll wear something really bizarre tomorrow just to piss you off you don't know me you wouldn't have a clue you don't care who i am or what i think or feel or know you just think tidy equals good well i don't give a tuppeny what you think where on earth am i supposed to be now where's that piece of paper that's right double english in 407 where the heck was that again i think it was down that long corridor near the courtyard now i'm late everyone will stare at me fabulous i wish i was back home good morning tuesday how do you do

WHAT ROSIE CAN SEE OUT THE WINDOW:

A very blue sky. Several clouds of the creamy, fluffy variety. The caretaker doing something sensible with hoses over on the far side of the oval. One abandoned brown schoolbag. The roses near the library all red and yellow and blowsy. Asher running down the corridor.

DOUBLE ENGLISH/A WORD FROM MR EPANOMITIS

Good morning, guys. Before we begin today I'll give back the assignments that you handed in yesterday. Yes, folks, don't faint, it's a miracle. In one night and one night only I did my marking. To be honest, I was only going to mark a few of them but I got quite engrossed. Some of them are very good indeed. I really liked the one by — here it is — Rosie Moon. She explored the idea of autobiographical writing by doing a present-day self and an imaginative fictitious one set in the past. Excellent. I also loved the one by someone with a wicked sense of humour. Wait on, where did I put it? Ah, yes, Thomas Corkingdale, a very funny glimpse into a warped mind, and all done in interior monologue. Sort of Billy Connolly meets *Mad* magazine. Great stuff, Thomas.

Now, while those are being given out let me tell you what we're going to be doing this morning. The first half of the class we'll be watching a video featuring four contemporary British poets, followed by a discussion. Then I'll get you to choose a partner and you can go off together to the library to research a poet and his or her work. Over the next few weeks each pair will be giving a five-minute class presentation on a poet of your choice. You can choose anyone from the Beat poets of the fifties onwards. Don't look so glum, lad, this will be fun, I tell you. No, Michael, they don't have to be British. Use your head, sunshine, the Beats were American. Now, wheel the television over here, and someone pull the curtains. Let's get this video happening.

I, THOMAS

I am Thomas McCorkingdale of the McCorkingdale McCorkingdales. You dare to ask about me and so it shall be. I have red hair and a red hat and sometimes I have red eyes but never on a Tuesday. I am, in the imperial, five feet ten in height but I do not have five feet. No, good sire, I have only two feet and two legs like all mortals but I am no ordinary mortal. No sire, for I am a McCorkingdale of the McCorkingdale McCorkingdales and we are not ordinary McCorkingdales. We come from far-off bonny Scotland, from the bonny McCorkingdale Isles, and it is there that I inherited from my bonny hairy forebears three amazing qualities that no ordinary non-McCorkingdale-type-person possesses, and well you may thank your lucky stars for that. And these three qualities are, in descending order of importance:

1. *The ability to drop toast onto fluffy carpet and have it fall butter-side down one hundred per cent of the time.*
2. *An unfailing talent for saying something totally unimportant during television programs at precisely the wrong moment so that the hapless listener will be prevented from hearing something crucial to the show.*
3. *A magical third ear. In addition to the two ears on the sides of the head, the three types of McCorkingdale (male, female and still undecided) have an extra ear protruding from the back of the left knee. However this ear only picks up every third word that is said, which can make the things they hear mighty mc-interesting.*

If you would like to know more about the McCorkingdale

McCorkingdales and how an evil curse was put upon our clan in the bonny hairy days of long ago, please turn to page 678, Volume IV of your bonny hairy Encyclopaedia Scotlandia.

ROSIE/TUESDAY/9.18am

I wonder where Asher was? Great shirt. I love the way he dresses. How long will he get away with it? I like Mr E. He's interesting, not uptight and snooty like Mrs Radisson was. Poets. I don't know any poets really, only old fashioned ones like Byron and Tennyson that we did last year. Look at his shoelace. He needs a new pair. Try not to stare at him. He does look good though. I wish I had dreads. Maybe I could ask him to be my partner. Oh, God, I couldn't. Move your head, moron, I can't see the video.

MR E

Good, class. I knew I could count on you lot for some lively debate. Well done for picking up on the fact that the themes of the Mersey poets are themes that are pretty universal and still relevant today: love, alienation, humour. Jake, could you hand out this sheet on research skills, thanks. Okay, guys, get yourselves a partner and go down to the library. Today I want you to pick your poet, see what information the library has about them and begin to make notes for the presentation. For homework I'd like you to find out what else you can from other sources, such as books at home, other libraries, etcetera. Off you go then, duckies.

ROSIE

Shall I? What have I got to lose? Just do it.

ASHER

oh damn here comes that girl i knew i shouldn't have winked at her she looks like such a try-hard she'll probably want to do some boring old fart quick who else can i go with no one yikes

FOUR THINGS ROSIE COULD HAVE SAID:

Hi, I'm Rosie.

Would you like to be my partner?

Hello, Asher.

I like your shirt.

ROSIE AND PIP/THE BEACH/ TUESDAY AFTERNOON

Come on, Rosie, tell me. It can't have been that bad.

It was worse.

Spit it out, baby.

All right, all right. Oh Pip, it was just so awful. Everyone else was grabbing partners and I started walking over to Asher, right? I was nearly there and when I looked at him he had this Don't Ask Me look on his face. But by then it was too late and I tripped over just as I got near him and then we both just stood there and neither of us said anything for ages. I just went totally blank. It was so awful.

Then what happened?

I said this terrible thing.

Yeah?

I can't believe I did this. I said, 'You'll get a dress pass.' I didn't mean to say it but I'd been thinking it and it just came blurting out. And he gave me this really filthy look and just stood there. It was like he thought I *wanted* him to get one. And then I asked him which poet he wanted to do and he said Jim Morrison.

But he's a singer.

That's what I said but he said that Jim Morrison was the finest poet of this century and I said that we wouldn't be allowed to and so he asked Mr E and he said sure and now we're doing him, Jim, I mean. And then we went to the library and there was only one book that had anything in it and we copied that down and then the bell went.

Did he say anything else?

Not really. At the end he said 'See ya' in this hope-I-never-do sort of way. Pip, stop laughing. It's not funny. Oh Pip, what am I going to do?

Well, Rosie, the way I see it is Jim Morrison is what you're going to do. Could have been worse, though. Could have been Elvis.

Pip!

Don't worry about it, Rosie. Stuff him if he wants to be standoffish. Come on. Let's have a swim.

MEET MALVINA

She's skinny. Tall. Quick, in speech and body. Wears big earrings shaped like birds or planes or dice or flowers. Dresses in colours soft and bright. Born in New Zealand. Came to Australia aged nineteen looking for adventure. Found it. Went to art school in the seventies, did sex and drugs and rock'n'roll inside out and upside down. Left Sydney, starring in a gypsy-queen road movie of her own creation.

Full of hope and raw enthusiasm, she helped to start Rainbowland community. Lived in a teepee. Fell in love with many men but ended up with Nigel of the long plait and kind hands, and made a baby with him under a full-moon sky. Grew round and full and lazy, queen of the vegetable gardens. Gave birth to a smiling boy and gave him a name which means the laughing one. For a while they stayed on at Rainbowland, the three of them, but things happened and in the end they gypsied on and put down roots of a kind in a town beside the sea.

A whole universe of days went by, summer followed spring and autumn danced past leading winter by the hand. Where did the years go? The kid got on with being a kid, gulping life with all his senses. He rode his bike and swam in the ocean and climbed tall trees. Malvina and Nigel lost a few dreams on the way but they thought — when they thought at all, between bringing in the washing and paying the phone bill — that they knew where they were headed. Yet somehow they woke up one day to burnt toast and regrets, face to face as strangers, just one too many late-night fights and carefully slammed doors. You can't say they didn't try. They tried okay, for the kid's sake, for their own sake, for the sake of love and kindness. In the end it all came down to dust and they said goodbye. And it's still very raw.

So here she is, Malvina, in a city far away on the edge of a desert where she hardly knows anyone, feeling about as low as a woman can feel. She's got a job in a bookshop that doesn't bring in much money, a seedy feeling in her guts from last night's companionship with a bottle of brandy, and no desire to go home and cook dinner. Malvina looks a lot better than she feels in her turquoise dress and her flying-pig earrings. She sits in Gino's cafe, drinking a luke-warm cappuccino and licking biscotti crumbs off her fingers. She is waiting for Asher, who, just in case you hadn't figured it out by now, is her son.

COFFEE BAR BLUES

Hi, Mum.

Asher. Hi. Sit here, love, I'll shift my bag. How was it?

How was what?

School, the second day of the dreaded school, how did it go?

Oh, God, it was wonderful. I can't begin to tell you.

That bad, huh?

Mmmm.

Want to tell me about it?

No. I hate it, that's all. I told you already.

It's always hard at first. A new place, fitting in.

I don't want to fit in. Sirens, dress codes, sit down and shut up. I hate it. I'd rather be dead than fit in there.

That bad, huh? Do you want a drink?

No, I had a Coke on the train. The English teacher is okay though. We have to do a presentation, in pairs, on a poet. He let me do Jim Morrison.

Wow. Good. Who's your partner?
Oh, this stupid goody-goody girl. I don't know her name. I think she wanted to do Lord Tennyson or some tedious old fart.
Tennyson's not so bad. 'The Lotus Eaters' is a good poem.
Yeah, Mum, right. Anyway we're not doing him. Can I get some chips or something? I'm starving.
No, Ash, we'd better get going. Payday is far far away. I'll make us cheese pancakes and salad as soon as we get home.
Yeah, okay. I need to plan my outfit for tomorrow.
Your outfit?
Don't worry about it, Mum. Come on, let's go.

NANA WRITES TO ASHER

Dear Asher,

I hope you are settling in well to life in Perth and the new school. Not giving the teachers too hard a time of it, ha ha. Grandpa and I are both well except for his new choppers. They look quite good but they don't fit properly. About three times a day I find him out in the shed rasping away at them with a file. He has to see the dentist again next week, if he has any plate left. He is persevering but I wouldn't be surprised to find the teeth shoved in the drawer one day soon. The rest of the time he is making some beautiful wooden boxes. One of them is for you. I have been going to my folk-dancing class and working in the garden. My tomatoes, corn and herbs are all doing well. Not much other news. Hot here, we get down to the beach to walk Lady most days. Say hi to Mum. The $5 is for your hot chip addiction.

Love from Nana

WHAT ASHER WORE TO SCHOOL/ WEDNESDAY:

Black woollen beanie with green marijuana leaf emblem on the front. Very, very old pair of greyish sneakers — which once upon a time were white — frayed canvas hole in big toe of both. Baggy dark-blue men's work trousers with ragged cuffs and two floral patches on bum. Long-sleeved Indian shirt, paisley muslin, in groovy shades of purple and olive green.

WHAT THE HOMEROOM TEACHER SAID

Dear Reader, I invite you to write this bit yourself. Invoke your imagination. Use the words disappointed, scruffy, and disgraceful.

WHAT THE HOMEROOM TEACHER DID

Gave Asher a dress pass.

WHAT ASHER FELT

Supreme satisfaction.

ROSIE AND ASHER/WEDNESDAY

There was no English class. At lunchtime Rosie saw Asher, sitting under a tree by himself eating a brown roll stuffed with cheese and salad, with hot chips on the side. Naturally she pretended she didn't see him. At exactly the same moment Asher looked up and saw Rosie and Pip walking past. Naturally he pretended not to see them.

WHAT ROSIE FELT

Embarrassed.

WHAT ASHER FELT

Embarrassed.

THE CALM BEFORE THE STORM

It is dinnertime at the Moon's house and Lily has made pesto: basil and garlic and olive oil and parmesan and pinenuts ground to a delicious green paste to stir through the pasta. There's a crispy salad in a big blue bowl, made with two sorts of lettuce, cubes of salty fetta and sweet cherry tomatoes. The fettuccine is nearly cooked and the table has been set with a white cloth and the decent plates — the blue speckled ones. There's a big bunch of cheerful sunflowers with dusty yellow faces, a round crusty loaf, a square of butter and an elegant Italian pepper grinder made of green glass.

The evening is hot and muggy, the sort of languid weather which proves that human beings are indeed descended from the three-toed sloth, but Lily is happy, despite the oppressive weather. She is proud of the meal she has made, and pleased that Robert has come home early for once and seems to be in a cheerful mood. She can hear him whistling as he waters the petunias on the patio. He's a good man, really, she thinks, maybe things will come right. Harry seems very perky. A while ago he scooted in and got some ice-cubes and scooted back out again in a very purposeful fashion. He's probably doing some little science experiment, Lily thinks idly. It's great when he does things, she thinks. She hates it when he just sits in front of the telly or the computer for hours on end. It makes her feel guilty, incompetent, a bad mother. But tonight she feels like a classically good mother, cooking a nice meal for her family and their guest. Rosie and Pip are up in Rosie's room, probably lounging around exhausted after their time at the beach. What a nice girl Pippa is, thinks Lily, a warm feeling spreading from her belly down to her plum-coloured toenails.

Lily drains the pasta, adds the pesto and a big handful of grated cheese, whirls the whole lot around. Bob, she calls, dinner's ready. Harry, she yells up the stairs, dinnertime. Tell the girls to come and get it.

ROSIE/LATER THE SAME NIGHT

I don't care. I'm glad I did it. Well, let Pip do it, then. Even though it hurt so much. Oh jeez, the pain. Better put some more tea-tree oil on it. Mustn't touch it all the time. It'll heal up soon, Pip reckons. Good old Harry, bringing up the ice and the matches to sterilize the needle, and not letting on to Mum what we were up to. It didn't work out quite like I expected, though. Quite a bit of blood really, and Mum calling and calling for us to come to dinner and us too scared to go down. Dad was good, though, sort of. He looked pretty startled when he came up to see what was happening and saw the bloodied tissues everywhere. But he did try to calm Mum down and see my side of it and that. She'll get over it. She can't make me take it out. It's my nose, after all. Hell, I hope it isn't so puffy in the morning.

School's going to be a bit of a stir. Thursday, what have I got? Human Biol, Double Art, Ancient History, Swimming, English. I bet Thomas McSmart-arse makes some dumb comment about my nose-ring. What am I going to do about the project? I haven't found out a thing. I wish I hadn't asked Asher to be my partner. I wrecked everything. Let's face it, there wasn't anything to wreck. He did seem neat, though, before he went all snobby. I think I'll wear my blue muslin dress. Flimsy and cool. Not really uniform but maybe I'll get away with it because it's blue. Great, The Cranberries. I love this song.

POSTCARD TO ASHER

Hi Ash,

Howz it going? Hope itz groovy. Schoolz hot and heaps of homework. Everyone misses you, especially me. Fuzzie had four kittens. They are so neat. Write to me!

kisses Jesse

WHAT ASHER WORE TO SCHOOL/ THURSDAY:

Black, red and yellow Bob Marley hat with a perky little brim. The world famous one-and-a-half lace green Docs. Grey corduroy trousers of the extremely baggy variety. Black-and-white striped short-sleeved pyjama top.

WHAT HE GOT

Yet another tight-lipped and tedious lecture. Dress pass number two.

HOW HE FELT

Terrific.

MR E

Seeing this weather is so ghastly I think we ll leave the room in search of coolness, guys. Go with your partners to the library or somewhere breezy in the grounds. Do not go home, up the street or to sleep. Sort yourselves out on the project, and come back in half an hour. I'll make up a list of presentation order. Thomas, I take that peculiar noise to mean you and Jake want to go first. Okay, scram. Be back here at three o'clock.

UNDER A TREE

Your nose . . .

Yeah, my friend did it.

The blue-hair girl?

Yeah, Pip.

Oh. Is it sore?

Pretty much.

They're cool though. My friend in Byron has one.

Oh. You know the other day?

Yeah.

I didn't mean I thought you *should* get a dress pass or anything. I like your clothes. I hate the stupid uniform thing.

Don't worry about it, it's cool. Anyhow, I've got two now.

Really?

Yeah, should get my third one tomorrow, right on schedule.

Then what?

Then I'll get sent to the headmaster, won't I?

Yeah.

Well, I couldn't give a tuppeny fuck.

Oh. Well, I didn't find out anything much about Jim Morrison.

I've got heaps. We can play the class some of his music and then talk about anarchy and rebellion. Look, I've done all this.

Well, what shall I do?

Do you listen to The Doors?

Not really. My dad said he thought he had a tape but then he couldn't find it.

You can come to my place if you want. On the weekend. Listen to some music and work out what we can each say.

On Saturday?

Yeah, in the afternoon. Here, I'll write my address on your arm.

FAMOUS SONGS OF THE RICH AND FAMOUS

ROSIE: Zombie

ROSIE'S FATHER: Messed Up in Mexico Living on Refried Dreams

ROSIE'S MOTHER: When a Man Loves a Woman

PIP: When I Come Around

HARRY: I'm an Arsehole

MR E: Prefers jazz

ASHER'S MOTHER: Moondance

ASHER: Anything by The Doors

WHAT EVERYONE DID THURSDAY NIGHT

Lily and Robert went out armed only with a credit card to try and form a meaningful relationship with a new lounge suite. Harry stayed over at Ted's house, and perfected the art of doing bombies in a suburban swimming pool. Rosie was supposed to do her homework but instead sploshed a little of her parent's gin into a glass of orange juice and then talked to Pip on the phone for twenty-seven and a half minutes. Pip watched *Home and Away*, made nachos and talked to Rosie on the phone. She felt vaguely jealous about Saturday but in truly heroic fashion offered her support, as in 'Good one, Rosie,' and some basic fashion advice, as in 'Wear that rainbow dress.' Asher ate two bowls of cold tuna mornay and five bits of watermelon and then he played 'Stairway to Heaven' over and over again on his guitar until it was time to watch the *X-Files*. Malvina did the grocery shopping, came home feeling grouchy, ate a cheese and tomato sandwich, had a lavender bath and went to bed to read *Women who Run with the Poodles*.

WHAT ASHER WORE TO SCHOOL/ FRIDAY:

His Kurt Cobain look-alike sneakers. Grey corduroy trousers of the extremely baggy variety. Once white t-shirt with faded Marilyn Monroe picture on front and hole in top right hand corner of front.

WHAT OCCURRETH

Verily Mrs Hyde said unto Asher, thou art a disgrace to the righteous amongst us for the scruffy and disobedient shall not inherit the classroom. Get thee to Mr McKenna and let his wrath descendeth upon ye.

AND YEA INTO THE OFFICE OF THE HEADMASTER WENT THE YOUNG ASHER

Come in lad, sit down, sit down. So, boy, Mrs Hyde has been telling me that you have made no effort to conform to our dress code and now I can see what she's talking about. Marilyn Monroe, *Some Like It Hot*, great film that . . . Anyway, ah hum, we do have dress regulations here at Birch Street and we expect all our students to conform to them.
Mmmm.
So, what have you got to say about it, Asher?
I don't believe in uniforms.
Don't believe in them, eh? Well, I know not everyone is in favour of uniforms but I'm afraid the rules are the rules and we just have to fit in whether we like it or not, lad. I expect you to do the right thing in future, do you understand me?
Mmm.
Right, off you go then, Allen.
Actually, it's Asher.
Oh.

WHAT ASHER MISSES:

The blue curve of Byron Bay. Creamy banana smoothies at the Lotus Cafe. Ditto the spicy cauliflower samosas. Riding his bike down towards the sea to get fresh bread and a paper on Saturday mornings. Reading the comics and eating wodges of fresh bread and vegemite on the verandah and feeding the crusts to the parrots. Sitting on the beach at sunset. Viv and Sam and Jesse. His father coming in after work and saying 'Let's go bodysurfing, Ash.' His old school. Lounging around under the gum trees at lunchtime, shooting the breeze with his friends, swapping food and talking. His falling-to-bits but brilliant tree-house. His father.

ALONE

stupid school stupid headmaster stupid everything don't need it don't want it got the blues got the black black blues got the shove your dress pass up your bum blues got the bruised everything is revolting blues gotta get out of here

WHAT EVERYONE DID FRIDAY NIGHT

Lily got hot and sweaty at aerobics. Robert worked late and then came home and sat on the patio and drank two lonesome beers. Harry got to the fourth level in 'Doom III'. Rosie and Pip were supposed to do their homework but instead they dressed up in strange outfits, using Lily's old clothes. Malvina went to a movie with Roger-from-work. Asher left town.

✉ THE NOTE THAT ASHER LEFT MALVINA

Mum, don't freak but I'm going back to Byron. I just can't hack it here. Don't worry about me. I'll ring you from Dad's.

I love you lots.

Asher.

PS. A girl from school will come around tomorrow afternoon. We were meant to work on our project. Tell her I've gone and that I'm sorry.

FRIDAY MIDNIGHT/MALVINA

God, how embarrassing. The one good thing about that job has been Roger. How could I not have guessed? Here I've been lusting after him daily for two weeks, and now, sadly, over hot chocolate and sticky-toffee pudding, he tells me he's gay and that he's still mourning Steve, his long-time lover, who died of AIDS last year. Just when I was wondering whether he and I might have a bit of a thing happening. Oh, well, he's such a nice guy. We can still be friends. Bit of a shortage of them on the ground around here. I knew that settling in to a new city would be hard but I didn't realise how awfully hard it would be. I guess it'll get better. Where's the door key? Should get me a huge funky key ring, always scrabbling around in this bag. Wonder if Asher is still up? Looks like he's out. Ah, he's left me a note. Oh, no.

☎ ONE SIDE OF A PHONE CALL

Nigel? It's me, Malvina. Something's happened. It's Asher. He's taken off.

—

No, well, not really. He didn't like the school much. It's pretty straight. But he seemed okay. It's midnight here. I just got home from a movie and found him gone. There's a note. He says he's coming to you.

—

I don't know. Maybe he's hitching. Or would he have got a bus across the Nullarbor? God, Nigel, he could be anywhere. It's thousands of miles. He's only fifteen. What are we going to do?

—

Do you think so? It seems a bit drastic but I guess we have to. I'll ring them now. Oh, Nigel, I hope he's all right. I'll ring you when I hear anything.

—

Yeah, okay. Bye.

FRIDAY MIDNIGHT/ASHER

mum will have the note by now she'll be freaking maybe i should get off go back no stuff it i just can't hack that school lonely don't belong rosie was the only good thing well mr e was okay darn it i can't get comfortable try to stretch legs out that's not going to do it try to rest head against window nope extremely uncomfortable elderly sleeping lady do you mind not leaning on me yo yo yo go ladies and gentlemen the total no-frills travel deal bad jokes from the driver and seats made for tiny little mutants hitching from sydney will be better no sweat how much money have i got left on me seventeen bucks that's heaps can always use my keycard all i have to buy is food if i hitch what will dad say he's got to let me stay jesse will get a surprise hey we're stopping roadhouse bright lights stretch legs get burger maybe chips and have a piss

SATURDAY/1am/MISSING PERSON REPORT

Asher Fielding. Fifteen years old. Male. Caucasian. Long dark brown hair worn in dreadlock style. 178cm tall. Slim build. Wearing blue trousers, green Doc Marten boots, possibly white t-shirt and black-and-white striped jacket. Category 25: Road, rail, bus. Headed for Byron Bay, New South Wales.

MALVINA/DRUNK/SATURDAY 2am

Asher, come back. Son, you are too young to go. You are dark curls and funny dreadlocks with bits of twig and fluff in them. You are smelly feet and the beginnings of a moustache. You are joy and sorrow and energy and boredom and earth and sun. You are Jim Morrison and Jimi Hendrix and oops your guitar string broke. You are heartbreak and loveliness and elbows and thumbs. You're just about all I've got in this strange desert town. Now you're gone, hitch-hiking away into the night on a dangerous adventure of your own design. I miss you. Send me a postcard. Be safe. Come home.

SATURDAY MORNING/ROBERT MAKES PANCAKES

Where's the sieve? Oh, way back there. Mug of flour. Whirl that sieve. Yo. Not a lump in sight. Just a little bit of sugar. Lily says not to put sugar in the mixture however I am king. Eggs, two, oops. Three mugs of milk. Rmmm, rmmm . . . me and my egg-beater. Look at that, smooth as silk. Bung it in the fridge while I find the other stuff. Lemon, halved. Brown sugar, yes.

Cinnamon, yep. Pan, ready. Sizzle a big blob of butter. Get goo from fridge, pour in pan, swirl around, hum Tom Waits song, wave egg-slice in air. Ah yes, brilliant. Who says I never cook?

ROSIE / SATURDAY MORNING

wakes late, sleepy-eyed, to slippery slinky sexy sunlight
half remembers dream of flying over bizarre flower garden
suddenly feels anxious, today being *a very special day*
gets up, has shower, washes hair, can't decide what to wear
tries on takes off tries on takes off tries on
finally decides Pip was right, yes, the rainbow dress
takes it off till later, hunts down silver bracelets
breakfast with Harry and Dad, three lemon pancakes yum yum
now what to do as ages still to go?
oops, Lily returns from walk, seems in bad mood, avoid her
go to room idly pick things up and put down again
Robert comes in has found old Doors tape, thanks Dad
plays music, writes down lyrics, makes sensible notes
decides Doors cool, Jim is very great poet, Asher was right
Lily comes in, says why aren't you doing homework?
says but I am doing homework
fights with mother
rings Pip but Pip not home
makes cup of coffee, eats four crackers with cream cheese and honey
turns on telly, no good, only sports
looks out bedroom window for extremely long time

inspects hair for split ends, finds many, snips off
called to lunch, not hungry, gets lecture on anorexia
says going out
goes through Spanish Inquisition
rainbow dress, red sandals, brushes hair, Sunflower perfume
mirror mirror, deep breath, just do it
rides bike to flat 3/79 Ivy Street

ROSIE MEETS MALVINA

Hi. I'm Rosie. Is Asher home, please?
Rosie. I'm Malvina. Oh, look, um, come in.

AND ROSIE IS THINKING

What a cool-looking mother. Mmm, neat flat, colourful pictures and books and interesting stuff everywhere. I wish I lived in a place like this, all messy and creative, not all has-to-be-perfect tidy yuppie Vogue Living like our house. Should I sit down or stand up? Where's Asher?

AND MALVINA IS THINKING

Rosie. So that's her name. What a beautiful girl. She has wonderful eyes. She's also very nervous. How the hell am I going to tell her?

ROSIE AFTER THAT

I can't go home yet. Mum will be right on to me like a vampire asking me what happened and I couldn't stand it. What will I do? Just walk around, I guess. I can't believe Asher ran away. He can't have been planning to or he wouldn't have invited me over. His poor mother. She said he might come back but she isn't sure. First they have to find him, then they have to sort things out. Maybe he'll stay with his father but Malvina said it was pretty unlikely because his father moves around a lot with his job. Asher must have really hated it here to just take off like that. I thought he liked me. His mother was great. She talked to me properly like I was an adult. What am I going to do? I can't just walk around all afternoon. Maybe I'll go to the markets and hang out till four-thirty and then go home. Damn you, Asher. I thought you liked me. Now I haven't got a partner. I'm still going to do Jim Morrison though.

ASHER/SATURDAY AFTERNOON

man will this ever end i promise i will never eat greasy sleazy yuck food ever again yes lord greasy grey hamburgers and cold rancid yellow things that once were chips will haunt my dreams for ever from this day forth it was just one truck stop too many big event of the day about to happen as we cross the border between western australia and south australia yes folks a major occurrence is about to break the monotony of the dusty highway here in eucla there's going to be a check for fruit as not a peach or pear can cross the mighty divide in case the dreaded fruit fly infests the crops notice many passengers now hastily gutsing down oranges apples bananas in order not to have to throw away a single bit yes and the bus pulls up and the fruit inspector gets on and what oh oh that other guy looks like he's a cop oh no he is a cop he said asher fielding here he comes plodding down the aisle damn it looks like i've been sprung

HANGING OUT AT FREMANTLE/ SATURDAY AFTERNOON

Tony's got techno pants and an undercut. He's trying to score a cigarette off Pete. Pete is shy, with fairly bad zits and a Mambo t-shirt and he's leaning against the wall trying to look sharp so that Lisa will come over and talk to him. Lisa has purple hair this week, really short and gelled up into little peaks, and she's asking Sara to lend her ten bucks so she can buy this really cool sixties silver Oroton purse from the second-hand stall at the markets. Sara is wearing a pink satin bodice and a cream lace fairy-skirt and she is hoping and hoping that Chris will show. Chris with the yin-yang tattoo does turn up but not for ages. He missed the bus because his old man made him mow the lawn. Sara and Lisa are going to Leon's party tonight. Lisa told her mother she was going to Sara's and Sara told her mother she was going to Lisa's. Here comes Pip.

LILY AND ROBERT TALKING/ SATURDAY NIGHT

I don't think we should have let her go.

Don't worry, Lily. She'll be fine.

I'm glad *you* think so. I don't feel good about it at all. It was so last minute, her and Pip rushing in like that, hassling us until we said yes. They never mentioned this party earlier. Who is this Leon anyway?

From what they said he sounds like a nice kid. I'm sure his parents will keep an eye on things.
We don't know that. We should have said no, or phoned them to check, or something.
I think you've got to let go a bit, Lily. Rosie's fifteen now, you can't wrap her in cotton-wool for ever. Do you want another beer?
No. Maybe you shouldn't have one either. You have to go and pick up the girls later.
For goodness sakes, Lily, lighten up. Two beers aren't going to push me over the limit.
I just worry, that's all. They could be getting up to anything at that party.
Come on, love, they'll be fine. Let's drag Harry off the computer and go for a walk on the beach.
Well, all right then. You get Harry and I'll get my shoes.

From LIVING WITH TEENAGERS

'TO BECOME INDEPENDENT AND MOVE SUCCESSFULLY INTO ADULTHOOD, ADOLESCENTS MUST LOOSEN THEIR TIES WITH CHILDHOOD, THEIR PARENTS AND THEIR HOME. THEY NEED TO TAKE RISKS AND TEST THEIR ABILITY TO MAKE THEIR OWN DECISIONS. THEY WILL RESIST MOVES BY THEIR PARENTS TO KEEP THEM DEPENDENT.'

THE PARTY

The music is Green Day and The Smashing Pumpkins, interspersed with The Beatles. The food is Mexican dip and corn chips and three large pizzas and a bowl of jelly snakes. The refreshments are Coca-Cola and a drink which began life as The Women's Weekly Economical Non-alcoholic Fruit Punch, courtesy of Leon's mother, but which has been transformed into Strange Tasting Woozy Weird Stuff by the addition of brandy that Tony nicked from home. It tastes foul but it's cold and wet and has floating strawberries and everyone is drinking it. There are also six bottles of Hahns Ice Beer that Rob got with the fake ID card that Julian got him in Thailand for five bucks; but no one wants to drink them as they are warm, because if Rob had put them in the fridge his parents would have said where did you get that beer? Mark is jamming away on Leon's guitar and Leon is very unconvincingly telling his dog, Marley, to go outside. Lisa and Lucy and Rosie and Pip are dancing, all glitter and glamour and whirling skirts. Sara and Chris are sitting on the back step with their arms around each other talking and eating jelly snakes. Then in comes Dave and Peter and Shelley and a couple of other kids that no one knows and not long after that everyone is sitting in a big circle passing around two huge joints that Dave got off Sam who got it from this guy in a nightclub in Northbridge. A total rip-off, guys, but hey, who cares? It's the real thing, and round it goes.

ROSIE THE MARIJUANA VIRGIN

I wasn't expecting this. What if Mum could see me now? It smells okay, very strong and herby. Pip says you have to hold the smoke down for ages but what if I choke and splutter? Everyone will know that I've never tried it. I don't want to look like an idiot. Yikes, Sam is puffing away like there's no tomorrow and then it's Lisa's turn and now it's me. Take it slowly. Act cool. Take a big deep drag.

ROSIE GROOVING/JUST AROUND MIDNIGHT

Thirsty. More punch. Whoa, spilled it. Doesn't matter. I've had heaps of punch but I'm still thirsty. My mouth is dusty and my tongue feels like a ping-pong ball. That's funny. Ping-pong ball. A conversation is very like a game of ping-pong, words flying back and forth. But without a table. How amazing. I must remember that. Yum, cold pizza. Tastes so good, all greasy and cheesy. Great song this, I just loooove this one. I feel like dancing. Where's Pip? Nooo, not here. She could be outside. I'll look for her. Oops, I'm a bit stumbly. Pip? No, that's Chris and Sara. And that is a gum tree. Hello, tree. And over there . . . oh darn, very dark out here, and I seem to be tripping over everywhere. And who's that over there? Oh, wow, it's Dad.

DRIVING HOME

So, was it a good party, girls?

Yeah, pretty good.

Quite a nice place they've got there.

Mmmm.

So, what does Leon's father do, do you know?

Not really.

Oh, you didn't meet his parents then?

No. They went to the movies.

Oh. So, good party then, was it?

Dad, you already asked that.

Well, you're not telling me much.

There's nothing to tell. Dad!

What?

Quick, pull over. I think I'm going to spew.

ASHER/SAME TIME/DIFFERENT PLANET

Back home now he is sleeping, still wearing his trousers, spread out like a rumpled sweaty angel, his dreadlocked hair tousled into seraph's curls. He dreams of a room full of glistening electric guitars and a pair of flying pineapples. He dreams of a sunset over a beach with a purple lace skirt where the sun should be, and a dusty road, and a hamburger dancing on two plump little legs.

Malvina stands in the doorway looking at him and trying not to cry because she was scared she was never going to see him again and because she knows how badly he misses his father, and damn it, so does she.

LATE SUNDAY NIGHT/NIGEL PHONES

Hello, Mal.

Nigel. I was just going to phone you.

God, it is so good that they found him. He get back safely?

Yeah, as I told you this arvo, the police picked him up at Eucla and bunged him on the next bus back to Perth.

So how is he?

I don't know. Subdued, I guess. He's mainly been asleep since then.

Well, that's understandable. How are *you*?

Fine. Terrible. I'm not sure what to do about the school thing. Whether to just send him back tomorrow. Whether to tell them what happened or not. Whether to try and get him into an alternative school, maybe.

What does Ash say?

I haven't talked to him properly yet. I wanted to give him a bit of space.

Right. Well, put him on, okay? I'll talk to you later.

Okay, I'll get him for you. Bye.

. . .

Hi, Dad.

Asher. The gypsy returns. You had us all worried there, mate.

Mmm.

So, what were the cops like?

Okay, I guess. They gave me a lecture about not wasting valuable police resources and not worrying my parents.

You did give us a bit of a fright.

I want to come back to Byron, Dad.

I wish you could, Ash, but it's not on right now. I'm going to be all over the place for the next few months.

I could do my own thing.

I don't think that's the best idea, son. Do you want to try another school?

Not really. I want to come back to Byron.

Look, I'm sorry, Ash, but it's just not an option right now. I doubt whether your mother would agree to it and I don't think it would be a good idea either, not with me away all the time. Do you reckon you could give the dreaded school another month or so? Settling in to a new place is always hard. Ash, are you there?

Yeah.

How about it?

I suppose.

Just for a month or two, hey? After that if it's still bad we'll sort something else out.

Yeah, okay.

I love you, Ash. I miss you, a lot.

Me too.

Look, I'll write to you soon. Put your mother back on, all right?

Yeah. Okay. Bye, Dad.

HOW TO MAKE DREADLOCKS

Don't wash your hair. Don't brush it. Occasionally twist, tease and fiddle with each dread, sculpting it into happy knotty bits, each of suitable weight and substance.

HOW NOT TO MAKE DREADLOCKS

Put wax on your hair. Pay $25 for each one at a posh hairdresser.

ROSIE/BEDROOM/SUNDAY NIGHT

Bloody mother. Carrying on and on. Silly old bag. Wasn't she ever young and fun-loving? Anyone would think that I was an axe-murderer or something. Not allowed to see Pip except at school for two whole weeks . . . not allowed to go to any more parties where no adults are present . . . not allowed to blah blah blah rhubarb rhubarb rhubarb. Just what I don't need when I'm feeling kind of seedy. Wouldn't have given her the satisfaction of knowing it but trying more mull or special punch wasn't exactly on my Must Do Right Away List anyway. Man, did I chuck . . . pity about my sandals. Hosing them down was fun though. I wonder if they'll dry funny?

God, I'm bored. Wish my nose would heal up. It's still so inflamed and gunky. I look dreadful. Good thing Asher isn't around to see me. But I wish he was. Wish my nose was better. Should put more tea-tree oil on it. Maybe I should take the ring out? Nah, wouldn't give *her* the satisfaction. They look really cool once they heal up. That shop in town has heaps of cute little nose jewels. I want to look really different. I wonder if I should do that thing Sara said with the wax. Dreads are wicked, I reckon. I think I'll do it. Melt up that old blue candle and rub it in. Dreads. Mum will have a fit but who cares?

ASHER'S BEDROOM:

Futon on the floor with black sheets and white pillows and a black doona. Row of books beside bed — arranged on board balanced on two bricks — including *The Hitchhiker's Guide to the Galaxy*, two Richard Brautigan books inherited from Nigel, and well-thumbed copy of *No One Here Gets Out Alive*, the Jim Morrison biography. One old guitar. Two songbooks. Three picks. Six white candles stuck in an assortment of bottles.

Ashtray in shape of crocodile. Photo of Asher, Sam, Viv and Jesse on a verandah, arms around each other, laughing. Batik backpack containing school books. Bamboo rack meant for holding clothes. Clothes on floor. Cassette player and twenty-seven tapes, four still with boxes. Poster of The Doors. *Pulp Fiction* poster. Sheep skull. Crystal pyramid. Empty sandal-wood incense packet. Half-eaten pear. And on the bed one lonesome boy.

INSIDE A LONESOME HEAD

here comes monday no way out i told dad I'd give it another shot so i suppose i have to i feel like an idiot didn't get very far wish mum wasn't so upset she's trying not to show it but i know she is she made macaroni cheese for dinner and spinach salad with pinenuts and an apricot crumble all my favourite foods but her eyes are sad i bet rosie is pissed off she won't want to be my partner now who cares who cares about any of it life basically sucks you get born get sick get old and die with zits and school and some boring old job in the middle think I'll play my guitar for a while god i wish dad was here i wish i wish god i don't even know what i bloody wish

ROSIE/LATER

Hell, they look weird. What am I going to do? Yikes, they're all waxy and bizarre. Help. I'd better ask Mum. No, she'll only lose it. No way I'm going to school like this. Maybe if I sleep on them the wax will crumble out and I can brush out the rest in the morning. Yeah, I'll just sleep on them. Can't be bothered cleaning my teeth. I'm so tired. Bloody school tomorrow. Wonder if Asher made it to Byron?

MONDAY MORNING BLUES OR MORE PRECISELY BLUE WAXES

For goodness sakes, Rosie, how could you?

You don't have to go on and on about it. Just help me get it out.

Stand still, will you.

Picking it off doesn't work, Mum. I've been trying that ever since I woke up.

Well, there's only one thing for it. I'm going to have to iron it off.

What?

Iron it off. I've removed candle wax from fabric like that. You lay the fabric on brown paper and when you iron it the wax melts and goes onto the paper. It's the only thing I can think of.

My hair, you'll burn it.

Not if I have the iron on really low. Come on. You can't go to school like that. Stop crying, Rosie. Come on, it'll be all right.

PIP AND ROSIE WALK TO SCHOOL/ MONDAY

Honestly, Rosie, you can't notice anything. It looks just like it always does.

True?

True.

Does it smell funny?

No, it smells fine, like shampoo.

When Mum ironed it it smelled all funny. That's why I washed it.

But my nose looks terrible, doesn't it?
Rosie, it's just a bit pink. They always get infected. Mine did. It'll heal up, couple of days max. Anyhow, how's your mother?
She was pretty furious, but she'll get over it. Isn't life just wonderful?
Yeah, right.
Look, there's Lisa and Sara. Come on, Pip, let's sneak up on them. I'm going to pick some of that bougainvillea and throw it at them. Pay Sara back for the beauty tip.
Rosie, you're nuts. Oh, all right then. Wait up.

MONDAY MORNING/STAFF ROOM/ BIRCH STREET HIGH

Mr E is having a strong cup of coffee, white with two. He's chewing happily on the apricot danish he bought on his way to school and reading his horoscope in the daily paper. He is half cynical and half believing about astrology. If the day's reading is gloomy he goes with cynical and tells himself that astrology is nonsense but if it's a good one he tunes in to his sensitive-new-age cowboy side and believes it. Today, for Taurus, it says that the day will be productive and uneventful, which seems boringly apt for a school teacher on a Monday morning.

The phone rings and he answers it — with his mouth full of apricot danish — and then has to swallow in a hurry so that he can talk to Malvina in a sympathetic and sensible way, like the professional sort of a person he is supposed to be. Mr McKenna, the headmaster, is at a conference and the guidance officer is with a parent, so Rhonda in the office thought he could handle this call since Asher is in his class. Sure, he tells Malvina. I understand. Thanks for letting us know. Yes, I'll keep an eye on him, treat him gently.

He gets off the phone feeling thoughtful. Poor kid. I didn't realise he was from interstate. Hell of an adjustment, new place, new school, separation of his parents. All that and adolescence too. What more could one kid have to cope with? It's a shame. He likes what he has seen of young Asher, the courage he showed wearing those funky clothes and challenging the rules, his zest for life with the Jim Morrison-as-great-poet thing. Well, he thinks, taking the last sticky delicious bite and licking his fingers, no day is ever entirely uneventful around here.

From LIVING WITH TEENAGERS

'During the teenage years parents should remember their primary role is gradually coming to an end. Soon they will no longer be responsible for their child's economic or emotional support. This is the time for parents to re-invest time and energy in themselves and their relationship. It is time to look to their own future without their child.'

LILY'S MONDAY MORNING

Tweeze eyebrows.

Shave armpits.

Use Epilady on legs.

Dishes, vacuum, washing.

Ring Sonia. Meet for coffee, Thursday?

Make appointment with therapist to discuss anxiety about Rosie.

Ring vet about Beethoven's itch.

Groceries. Health food shop. Organic vegies.

Bank. Take in dry cleaning. Buy stamps.

Aerobics, 11 am.

Get home in time to watch the 'Midday Show'.

MONDAY MORNING/ROBERT DRIVES TO WORK

He's playing an old Pink Floyd tape really loud on his car stereo and remembering way back to the sixties when the whole world felt exciting and good and wondering why Lily is always so crabby and anxious these days and whether his morning client will show and should he perhaps not have worn the floral tie with the green shirt and maybe he'll have salad for lunch at Cafe Rialto although what he would rather have is a nice fattening cheese and bacon toasted sandwich from the little deli and how come weekends are so short and how come he feels so goddam old . . .

SO THEN WHAT HAPPENED WAS

Rosie arrived early for her English class. She wanted to talk to Mr Epanomitis about how she was going to have to do her poetry project without a partner, but all she found was a class-room empty except for thirty-seven desks, one rubbish bin, one abandoned sports sock and four bits of scrumpled paper. This was because Mr E was stuck in the staff room asking Mrs Hyde to lay off Asher about his clothing and give the lad a bit of a chance to settle in. Mrs Hyde grudgingly said she would, mainly because she knew she was fighting a losing battle against a plague of scruffiness that was overtaking the entire planet and, moreover, most of her thoughts were focused on the fact that this was Monday and she had just begun another boring diet and all she had to look forward to at lunchtime were four Ryvitas with cottage cheese, a few slices of tomato and a rather small apple.

Then in came Thomas and Michael and Lucy and Shannon and Emma and Hannah and Sam and Leon and Mr E and Val and Bonnie and Purdie and Scott and Victor and Anna and Julia and Amy and Tim and Emily and Jeff and Sara and Michael and Ben and Paul and Kay and Harry and Jake and Michelle and Clare and Sophie and Nick and Simon and Chris and Maria and Bea and Tony. They were making quite a racket. Rosie was so busy thinking about the weekend and drawing stars and clouds on her folder cover with a red Texta that she wasn't taking much notice of anything, so when Asher came in and plonked himself down beside her and she looked up and saw him she was very surprised indeed, dear reader, as well you might imagine.

MR E

Welcome to Monday, ladies and gentlemen. Did any of you get to see the Brett Whiteley exhibition on the weekend? Great stuff. I recommend you go along and see it if you can. He was such a talented artist, quite phenomenal. There was a beaut t-shirt for sale with a Whiteley quote on it: 'Life is brief but

Thursday afternoon seems very long indeed.' Transpose that to Monday morning and there's my freshly borrowed thought for the day. But let's make the best of it.

What I'd like you to do is to get out the handout I gave you last week, those examples of contemporary poetry. Have a look at the poems for five minutes or so and also re-read the notes you made when we talked about modern poetry, themes, forms, stylistic devices, all that sort of thing. Then I'd like you to write a poem, and see if you can capture the essence of what we've been talking about. A good way to learn about a writing style is by imitating it. Thomas, my man, get that look of horror off your face. It's supposed to be fun. Try a parody if you like, lad, a bit of tongue-in-cheek will be fine — use your wonderful talent for humour. Any topic will do, and if you're really stuck there's always the old chestnut of 'My Weekend'. Okay, settle down and get started, guys. For anyone whose memory needs a boost I'll put the definition of parody up on the board.

THE NOTE

??????

hi   sorry about Saturday   i took off

I know, your mother told me   Hey wot happened?

mum rang the cops & i got sprung at Eucla

Shit

double shit and hello planet perth . . . will you still be my partner for the assig??

Yes, *if* you don't take off without warning.

okay   it's good to see you

Ditto. Talk to you after class — we gotta write poems.

HIGHWAY by Asher Fielding

travelling the white line
into the night

gypsy blues
bus station homesick blues
cold chips and luke-warm coffee blues
lonesome midnight adventure blues

destination anywhere
travelling the white line
into the night

FIFTEEN by Rosie Moon

i am fifteen i am nose-ring
i am fifteen i am roses at sunset
i am fifteen i am happy sad and in-between
i am fifteen i am docs and lace and feathers
i am fifteen i am cloud and earth and moonbeam
i am fifteen i am rosie i am changing
let
  me
    fly

PARODY: A mocking imitation of the style of a literary work, ridiculing the stylistic habits of an author or school by exaggerated mimicry.

DOING THE AUSTRALIAN HOWL

by Thomas Corkingdale

(A parody of 'Howl' by Allen Ginsberg)

I saw the best minds of my generation destroyed by vegemite pepsi and nobby's nuts, fat zitty wasted,
dragging their cars down ugly car-yard highways looking for a chicken treat
technoheaded popsters yearning for an instant wonderful connection to cyberspace reality
who red-eyed and penniless sat up watching eat carpet waiting for the angry parent morning
who wandered aimless from shopping mall to supermarket searching for something that wasn't made of plastic
who swam recklessly in chlorine pools under melanoma sunlight praying the new-age angel of death would spare them
who had their dreams and visions starved by parental words of not now and maybe later
who survived mondays only to find tuesday lurking crazily behind their neon backsides
who lived only for the joy of reebok nike and mambo
smashingly pumpkined out of their minds on wonder bread and no-name peanut butter

with the absolute hell of adolescence tortured into their
happily wasted minds for ever

DINNERTIME AT THE MOON SITE

Watch that juice, Harry, you'll knock it over. You seem very cheerful, Rosie. How was school?
Okay.
Anything exciting happen?
Um, we wrote poetry in English.
That's nice, dear. Oh no! Harry, I *told* you that would happen. Quick, someone grab a cloth.
Sorry, Mum.
Do try and be more careful, will you?
What did you do today, Lil?
Oh, nothing, darling. Just the usual. Who'd like more lasagne?
I would, Mum.
No thanks. Not for me, hon.
Mum, please can I leave the table? I want to go over to Pip's to do some homework.
Rosie, I told you, you can't see Pip for two weeks—except at school.
Please, Mum. This is different. This *is* school, kind of. We have to work on our project. It's due in soon. Please.
I think that would be okay, don't you, Lil?
Well, oh, all right then. When will you be home?
Um, by nine-thirty. Hey, thanks, Mum.
Mum, can I leave the table too? I want to watch 'Seinfeld'.

I suppose so. God, Robert, you never back me up over things. I just don't get any support when I try to discipline the kids.
Come on now, Lily. You know that's not true.
For goodness sake, what about what happened just then? I say she can't go and you just come right on in and undermine me.
Oh, for the love of pete, what the hell are you on about? She's only going to Pip's to do her homework.
It's the principle of the thing. We should present a united front.
Well, I don't think so. Why on earth should we have to pretend we agree when we don't. Anyway, I'm going to watch 'Seinfeld' with Harry. Coming?
No.

LILY WASHING UP

I hate him. He just doesn't care about me and my needs at all. He just goes off and leaves me with the dishes. All that effort to make lasagne and then everyone just gobbles it down and leaves me to clean up. It's not fair.

ROBERT WITH HALF AN EYE ON 'SEINFELD'

She's driving me nuts. She doesn't want to know about the way I see things. Nothing I do is ever good enough. And then she makes a big deal about staying in the kitchen and doing her martyr act with the dishes. Couldn't they wait for once? Can't we ever just relax and enjoy ourselves?

HARRY

Why do they always have to fight? I wish Mum would come in here and just hang out with us.

ROSIE AND ASHER MEET IN THE PARK/7.25pm

Hi.

Hi.

You made it.

Yeah. I told Mum I was going to Pip's place to do some homework.

Don't your parents let you go out much?

No. Well, kind of. Dad's pretty cool but my mother isn't. She always wants to know where I'm going and who with and all that stuff. I'm not supposed to be seeing Pip right now except for at school, anyway.

How come?

It's a long story.

Tell me?

Well, when I went to your place on Saturday and you weren't there I didn't want to go straight home, so I headed down to the markets to hang out and I met Pip and all these kids from school and we got invited to this party. My mum didn't really want me to go because she didn't know Leon, it was his party, right, but in the end she said yes. Anyhow my dad came to pick me and Pip up at midnight and on the way home I spewed everywhere and Mum got really freaked out because there weren't any adults at the party and she thought I'd been drinking.

Had you?

Yeah, a bit. And the rest.

Like what?

Well, I had my first smoke of dope.

Oh.

You probably do it all the time, right?

No, not really. There's a lot of it around in Byron so I've done it a bit. It's no big deal. My parents used to do it a lot but they don't any more. Now Dad meditates and Mum drinks wine.

Wow. Your parents did it?

Yeah, sure. Didn't yours?

No way. Well, I doubt it. They don't tell me stuff like that.

Oh. What time do you have to be home?

Nine-thirty.

So shall we go back to my place and do stuff on our Doors project?

What will your mother say?

Probably hello, do you guys want a cup of something?

Well, yeah, all right then.

Cool.

ROBERT GOES TO BUY ICE-CREAM/ 7.45pm

I hope they have butter pecan. Chocolate is okay but butter pecan is the best. Thank goodness Lily loosened up. I'm glad she came in to watch the end of 'Seinfeld', and that Harry asked for ice-cream. This is what life is meant to be, good times and treats, not fighting and blaming. Maybe things will work out. It has been precarious lately. Come on, mate, watch what you're doing. Ah ha, a Volvo driver, that'd be right. Look out, you two on the bicycles, you're too young to die. Hey, that's Rosie. And that sure as hell ain't Pip.

ROSIE AND ASHER AND JIM MORRISON

They are cruising in Asher's room, enjoying the music and the company and the hot chocolate with marshmallows that Malvina made. It's 'Riders on the Storm' and words that mean something and great guitar playing and trying to look cool when you feel shy. There's a soft night breeze making the curtains dance and a smell of frangipani from the tree outside the window mixed with a strong smell of malt from the factory down the street. And Rosie is thinking — gee he's nice and maybe I'll ask him how he did his dreads and I hope my nose doesn't look too revolting and I wish I didn't have to go home soon. And Asher is thinking — I like her a lot and her hair is beautiful and she smells like flowers and I wish I could write lyrics like Jim could and maybe Perth isn't so bad after all and I wish she didn't have to go home soon.

ROSIE AND ASHER CYCLING HOME

That was fun.

Yes, it was. So are we ready to give our presentation or what?

Yeah, I reckon. We just need to get Mr E to arrange a cassette player for us.

Mmm. So, we'll play 'The Poet's Dream' first and 'Riders on the

Storm' second and then we'll both read our pieces out and finish with 'An American Prayer'. Let's see if we can do ours next and get it over with. I'll put the tape in my schoolbag.

Fine by me.

Asher?

What?

If you had a band what would you call it?

I don't know. Why?

Well, it's just that I think bands' names are great, that's all. Sometimes lying in bed at night I make them up, just for fun.

Tell me some.

You won't laugh?

No. Well, not unless they're funny.

Okay. Screaming Numbats. The Purple Honeysuckles. Warped Minds. Mermaids in Drag. Spewbuckets. Stuff like that.

Right. Hey, Stuff Like That would be a good name for a band, too. What about The Grovellers?

Imaginary Crimes.

Zoo Mutants.

Total Fucking Strangers.

Yeah, that's a good one. Do you know what I do, late at night in bed?

What?

I plan trips. For when I leave school. I think about getting a car with some of my friends, travelling around Australia, stopping where we like, no destinations, having adventures. Or getting some money together and setting off, hitch-hiking, India,

America, anywhere. Downtown the world, Malvina calls it.

I like that, downtown the world. My life feels so opposite to that most of the time. More like uptight the suburbs.

Oh?

Yeah, well, my parents aren't getting along that well. My mum is very uptight about everything. No is her favourite word and anxiety is her drug of choice. And school is so straight and restrictive most of the time.

You said it. You know, I was wrong about you.

What do you mean?

When I first met you you seemed like . . . well . . .

What? Go on, tell me.

Well, don't get pissed off with me but you looked pretty straight, a bit of a try-hard. Someone who did what she was told, never made waves.

I'm not like that.

I know.

Here's my house. I'd better go straight in. I'm a bit late.

Sure. See you at school then.

Yeah.

Yeah, well, see ya then.

INSIDE HIS HEAD

maybe i shouldn't have said that about thinking she was a try-hard i hope she isn't mad at me you never can tell with girl creatures but she seemed to understand hey cat i nearly flattened you she's fun making up those names was cool i want to see her again not just in school and let's face it man you really like her

ROSIE

That was ace. He is *so* gorgeous. I wish he hadn't thought I was a Miss Goody Two Shoes, though. I bet all the girls in Byron Bay are all groovy hippie chicks. I wonder if it's too late to ring Pip and tell her all about it? Yikes, it's nearly ten o'clock. Don't let Mum be mad. Oh good, they're watching telly. Maybe if I just slide in quietly . . .

THE SHIT HITS THE FAN

The telly goes off and the ominous words are said. 'Come and sit down, please. We want to talk to you.' Rosie can sense the tension in the room and her belly tightens, her body knows that here-comes-trouble feeling. So Robert tries to begin calmly and carefully, but before Rosie has a chance to put her case and claim her life as her own, Lily is up and running with words like lying and dishonesty and boundaries, and voices are raised and no one wants to listen to how it really is to be fifteen and surrounded by the word no, and things get out of control and shouting takes place and doors are slammed and there she is, Rosie, sprawled on her bed with her face in the cushions, weeping, weeping.

NIGHT PASSED & PEOPLE SLEPT & SO ENDED A RATHER BIG MONDAY

TUESDAY MORNING/BREAKFAST WITH A CONTROL FREAK

Lily carefully smears a tablespoon of ricotta cheese (40 cals) onto a piece of wheat-and-yeast-free rye toast (70 cals) and adds a teaspoon of sugarless strawberry jam (40 cals). She quarters a small pear (70 cals) and slices a medium small nectarine (40 cals) and puts them on the green plate with the toast, fossicks for a women's multivitamin supplement with added iron and calcium (no cals) and pours a cup of Irish Breakfast tea with a slosh of skim milk (10 cals). Lily prefers to think in calories instead of kilojoules because those are the numbers that lodged in her brain when she was sixteen and first digested the idea that beautiful equals thin. Also calories sound less than kilojoules, which can run into three figures for something as innocent as a muesli bar (704kJs!).

Lily is nervous. At eleven o'clock she has an appointment with a therapist, Dr Parker, in West Perth. All the women at the tennis club have been talking about Dr Parker and how wonderful she is. Lily has been wanting to talk to someone for ages about Rosie and their relationship. How fortunate I got that cancellation, she thinks, and how amazing the timing is, after that ghastly blow-up last night.

What shall I wear, Lily wonders? The blue frock? No, I wear that everywhere. The white suit? Too dressy. The brown shift? Too tight. What about the flowery skirt and the black silk shirt? Yes, that might do it. With the black sandals and the garnet earrings . . . yes. I'll get ready now, thinks Lily, and then I'll have time to stop off and do some errands on my way.

ROSIE AND PIP WALK TO SCHOOL/ TUESDAY

It is a blue sky sunny morning and the whole world is smiling: rose bushes, dogs, letterboxes. Rosie tells Pip everything and Pip is envious and delighted as well, except about the parental blasting of which she has copped a serve recently herself for not being responsible about chores blah blah blah and rhubarb. They agree that parents are boring old farts and that this day would be far better spent at the beach and that Rosie's nose is nearly normal now and that getting two chilled Cherry Ripe bars from the deli is a good idea and that this singing dancing hug-me-baby feeling that Rosie is having is probably that mysterious thing called love but that if she doesn't shut up about Asher then Pip is well within her rights to cause serious bodily harm with a flying schoolbag.

LILY MEETS DR PARKER

So, Lily, what brings you here?

Well, it's about Rosie, my daughter. She's fifteen. We've always got along really well but this last year things have really deteriorated. We fight, she won't talk to me, and she has begun doing all sorts of totally unacceptable things.

Tell me about that.

Well, she got her friend to pierce her nose and put a nose-ring in. It just looks dreadful.

Dreadful?

I just think they look awful, unsightly. This dirty grunge look, I don't understand it. I mean, what's the matter with being clean and tidy?

Do any other of your daughter's behaviours concern you?

Yes, well, I think she's experimenting with drugs and alcohol. Last weekend we let her go to an unsupervised party and on the way home she vomited. I think she was drunk or something worse.

Worse?

High on marijuana.

Ah. Is there anything else that's troubling you?

Well, yes. Last night she said she was going to her best friend's house to do some homework. My husband went out to get some ice-cream and he happened to see her hanging around the streets with a boy.

So did you talk to her about this?

Well, we tried to but the whole thing just escalated and ended up with Rosie storming out and locking herself in her bedroom.

Oh, I see. Lots of difficult times for you lately.

Yes, you could say that.

Any other children?

I have a son, Harry, he's eight.

So how are things going with him?

Okay, I guess. He's pretty active and a real computer addict.

Mmm. And do you have a job outside the home?

No, I'm a housewife. I was an admin assistant for a firm of accountants before I had my kids.

Okay. Now, Lily, what about you, your own life, how is *it* going? Tell me about your hopes and dreams, your relationship with your husband, anything that's relevant. Give me a picture of you.

There is silence. A long silence. And then sobbing.

Lily? Here, have a tissue. So, maybe what's been happening with your daughter is not the only issue here. But it *is* often a gritty time when teenagers break away and begin to establish themselves as people.
It's like I've lost her and we're no longer friends.
Yes, as parents we feel rejected and it hurts. Yet your daughter is doing what she needs to do, moving out into the world and away from you. It's normal. Now could be the time to live your own dreams. Lily, I think we could do some useful work together. Are you ready for this journey?
Yes, I am.
Once a week, then, for now. Does this day and time suit you?
Fine.
All right then. You might like to begin using a journal as a safe way to begin to explore: drawings, feelings, quotes, anything. Make time for three things each day that are just for you, not for your husband, your children or anyone else, things that you find pleasurable. Things you haven't done much of lately perhaps. Okay?
Yes.
Well, until next Tuesday then.

TUESDAY AT SCHOOL

This is as good as it gets. Thomas Corkingdale and his partner don't have their presentation prepared so Rosie and Asher do theirs and it is brilliant and everyone loves it and Mr E is rapt and says you have set a very high standard and good on you, guys.

At lunchtime Pip and Rosie and Asher sit together under a tree on the oval and at first being a threesome is shy and awkward, but after a while it mellows out and they eat peanuts and goof off and make up some more band names, and after lunch even Ancient History seems fascinating, angels dance above the school and all is right with the world. And if you want to know what the bands' names are, well, here they are.

The Chapter

Travellers

The Trip

Spanner and the Dog

The Godless

DOCTOR PARKER'S MEDICINE/ TUESDAY/AROUND NOON

Lily sits in a cafe and orders a cappuccino and a piece of orange halva cake with cream. To hell with the calories. She sits at the outdoor table and relaxes, feeling the sun on her skin. She stares at the other customers and invents whole new lives for them. The man with the silver ponytail and the mobile phone is definitely a cocaine dealer, even if he thinks he is a boutique owner. She reads glossy magazines greedily. To hell with the grocery shopping. She buys two journals with wonderful covers, one for her and one for Rosie. She goes home and makes a fried egg on buttery vegemite toast and reads her book on the patio. To hell with the housework. She drifts off to sleep and dreams she is dancing on a cloud in a red swimsuit and red shoes that are studded with tiny sparkling jewels.

AFTER SCHOOL/TUESDAY/LILY AND ROSIE

Hi, Mum.
Hi. Good day?
Not bad. Pretty good actually. Asher and I did our presentation in English.
Asher?
The guy Dad saw me with. He's new. From Byron Bay.
Oh, right. What was the presentation about?
Jim Morrison, his song lyrics as poetry.
Oh, interesting. Did I ever tell you that Dad and I went to a party soon after we met and the song we danced to all night was 'Light My Fire'. Someone told us later that after everyone went home the sofa we had been sitting on burst into flames. Someone had probably left a cigarette butt in it or something. It seemed pretty amazing at the time.
Yeah, for sure. I can't imagine you and Dad dancing to 'Light My Fire'.
We weren't always old fogies, you know. Hey, I bought you something today.
What?
A journal, to write in. Here, look.

That's great. How come there's two?

I got one for me, as well. Oh blast, there's the phone. Stir this for me, will you?

ROSIE THINKS

How weird. I can't remember when she was in such a good mood. I wonder what this is . . . cheese sauce or something . . . maybe she's making that spinach souffle thing Dad likes. Goodie, I always wanted a journal but I'm going to hide it for sure in case it's a trick and she just wants to find out all my secrets. Can't be too careful. Hide it where, though? Behind the books in my bookcase? Nah, I know. I'll do that thing that Pip's brother did where you cut the inside out of a big book and hide things in there. Yes, that's what I'll do. I could do it with that big horse book. Perfect.

✉ POSTCARD TO ASHER

*Hello Groover ******

Howzit going in the evil city of Perth? I named my kittens Squashblossom, Kurt, Marble and Fifi. I want to keep them but Mum says to find them good homes. No way. Sam broke his wrist skateboarding. What a bummer, hey? Everyone is amazed 'cause your dad is going out with Eli's mother. Truly weird! Write to me. I miss you heaps. Just Do It. *jjjjjjjjjjesse xoxoxoxox*

A NASTY TWIST OF FATE

Asher does not look in the letterbox. He has more important things to do. It's been a great day and he is happy. First he makes himself a bowl of cereal with cold milk and brown sugar and then he washes down a few handfuls of corn chips with a tumbler of orange juice. Next he gets on his bike and pedals madly down the street, off to the beach to look for shells and dried seaweed so he can do some sketches of natural objects for his art assignment. Then he comes home and pours another orange juice and eats a couple of leftover cold potatoes and puts his feet up in front of the telly for a spot of veg-out heaven.

So it's Malvina who, arriving home tired from a particularly bad day at the bookshop, checks out the letterbox. One power bill, a leaflet from Dial-A-Pizza, and the postcard. She's not a snoop, Malvina, but as she trudges up the path she can't help but, well, not *read* it exactly but more sort of glance at it really and man, is she pissed off.

MOONSVILLE / TUESDAY / 6pm

Robert comes home and Lily greets him with a hug and a smoochy kiss. Harry says, 'Dad, I made mango jelly for dessert, and Mum made that spinach thing.' 'Whack-oh, little buddy,' says Robert and he goes to have a shower. On the way through the lounge he sees his daughter, sprawled out on the floor, scribbling away at something.

What are you up to, Rosie?

I'm writing in my new journal. Mum bought it for me.

As Robert lathers up with the green soap that smells of forests and oceans, he whistles 'Love Me Do' as loudly as he can and realises that he is happy from head to toe. No need to win Lotto, go to Bali or win the Citizen of the Year award. To come home to Lily and a bit of a cuddle and happy kids and a good meal is all he ever asked for. Nothing fancy. A simple kind of happiness, plain and true.

HARRY TELLS A JOKE AT DINNERTIME

Well, this man went into a bar and he met a woman and she asked him to come back to her place for some kinky sex and then they went back to her place and they took off all their clothes. Then the man started running around the room and he was naked and he was flicking the light switch on and off and yelling, 'Lightning, Lightning.' And then he ran around the room farting and he was yelling out, 'Thunder, Thunder.' And then he ran around the room yelling, 'Raining, Raining' and weeing in the corner. And then he did them all together – 'Lightning, Thunder, Raining, Lightning, Thunder, Raining.' And then he put on his clothes and started to go home. The lady said to him, 'I thought we were going to have some kinky sex' and the man said, 'Hell, no, not in this dreadful weather.' Get it? Mum, what does *kinky* mean?

FLAT 3/79 IVY STREET

No spinach souffle and no laughter. Malvina hands Asher the postcard with a scowl as if it is a piece of fresh dog-shit and even before he reads it he knows it has a bad-luck feel about it. Then he reads it and he feels lousy in twelve different ways, which are:

1 Guilty about not having written to Jesse
2 Appalled at his dad for going out with Eli's mum, whom he remembers as being kind of twitty, all lipstick and giggles and orange and pink clothes
3 Upset that Malvina is upset
4 Protective towards his dad, but only sort of
5 Confused
6 Rejected
7 Homesick
8 Guilty about liking Perth
10 Guilty about liking Rosie
11 Worried about how Malvina will react
12 Totally pissed off with everyone and all of it

SO HOW DID MALVINA REACT?

Oh, imagine it, dear reader. She stayed furious and clumped crabbily around the kitchen for a very long time indeed, yet produced only baked beans on somewhat blackened toast. She poured herself a large glass of wine and spent the next half hour drinking it and listening to old Van Morrison tapes and staring out the window. Then she poured another one. When Asher tried to talk to her she was snappish and peevish and they both went grumpily off to bed.

POSTCARD TO JESSE

Hi. Sorry I haven't written, my fingers fell off . . . The kittens sound neat, send me one? My school is mainly crappy but I have made two friends, Pip and Rosie. Perth is so different from Byron, it's a sprawly straight place but Fremantle is groovy, markets and coffee bars and buzz . . . you would like it. We are living in a flat near a pickle factory and Mum has a bookshop job. Say hi to Viv and Sam for me. Miss you all and surfing.

xoxoxox Ash

PS. Excuse the smudge. It's Vegemite, I'm having breakfast.

IF YOU WERE AN ANIMAL WHAT WOULD YOU BE?

ROSIE: a unicorn

ROSIE'S FATHER: a wild black horse

ROSIE'S MOTHER: a siamese cat

PIP: a sea bird

HARRY: a millionaire's pet puppy

MR EPANOMITIS: thinks it's a flaky question

ASHER'S MOTHER: a dragon

ASHER: a tiger

WEDNESDAY

Uneventful. Breakfast, lunch and dinner were prepared and eaten by everyone you have met thus far, except that Mrs Hyde had a liquid diet-drink for lunch, which was all that she deserved. The culinary highlight of the day was a sandwich invented by Harry which consisted of white bread spread with both chocolate-nut paste and honey and then sprinkled wildly with cornflakes. Strangely, he forgot to add alfalfa sprouts.

Office and tennis club and bookshop were attended by respective parent-type people and school by everyone else. A little housework got done at Rosie's house but not a lot, and none at all at Asher's, not even the dishes.

Pip and Rosie and Asher spent lunchtime lying on their backs on the oval with their faces in the shade and their feet in the sun, improvising on the theme of 'when we leave school and have an awfully big adventure'. They discussed at length whether getting a Volkswagen kombi van would be a better idea than a Holden station wagon, and did not even attempt to solve the zen koan of who was going to fund the expedition.

Harry lost a tooth and scored a dollar but let us not even pretend that we think the tooth fairy gave it to him.

All in all, an ordinary sort of a day.

MR McKENNA/THE STAFFROOM/ THURSDAY

I'm sorry to call this emergency meeting, people, but something very important has come up. Yesterday afternoon, before Mrs Hyde left the school, she found that her wallet had been stolen. It contained quite a large sum of money, around $130, plus her credit cards and driver's licence, etcetera. Understandably Wendy is pretty upset about it, even more so because she feels she has a fair idea who took it. I'll be looking into the matter but meanwhile I'm letting you all know so that you can keep a good watch on your valuables. Please don't leave anything unattended in the classrooms. Make use of your pigeonholes in the staff room. Also I want you to keep your ears to the ground and get back to me if you hear anything relevant. Similarly I'll keep you all informed. Right, then. Back to work, team. Can I see you in my office for a minute, please, Tim?

MR McKENNA TALKS TO MR E

Tim, let me get straight to the point here. Wendy seems to think that the new lad, Asher Fielding, has taken her wallet.

Oh, really? What grounds does she have for this assumption?

Well, she says he's a very sullen and rebellious boy, a difficult character . . . and that this is his way of getting back at her about the clothing incident.

Does she have any proof?

No, not really, although she seems to remember he was the last one to leave the classroom yesterday morning. She says she noticed him lagging behind in the corridor as she left the classroom to go to the toilet. Her wallet was in her drawer and it could have gone missing then, although she didn't actually notice it was gone until the afternoon.

Pretty silly place to leave a wallet.

Yes, but that's not the point, Tim. The wallet has been stolen. It's a serious matter and we have to deal with it as such. Now, what do you think of young Asher? He's in your English class, I believe, and the admin log book says you took a call from his mother last week.

Yes, I did. Look, Asher seems a good kid to me, bright, responsive, creative. His mother phoned to say that he has been through a lot lately. She just wanted me to know he might be feeling sensitive, keep a bit of an eye on him.

Been through a lot? Such as?

Well, actually, he ran away. Got on a bus and headed for Byron Bay where his father lives. Apparently the parents broke up fairly recently and the boy was homesick, missing his dad. He didn't get far. The police found him at Eucla and sent him back.

Police involvement. Hmm, I think I'd better have a word with young Asher.

Look, Ed, I really don't think it would have been him. In my opinion he's a good kid. There are thirty or so other kids in that class. It could have been any of them.

Leave this one with me, all right, Tim? Back to work now, please.

ROSIE'S JOURNAL/THURSDAY NIGHT

Today something dreadful happened. Asher got called in to Pinhead McKenna's office and accused of stealing Mrs Hyde's purse. The silly old cow can't stand him, just because he wears cool clothes and dared to challenge her control-freak mechanisms. Asher told Mr Mac that he didn't do it but he didn't feel like he was believed. They can't prove anything so he just got a long lecture and was told that 'returning the stolen goods would be the appropriate thing'. How can he return the bloody thing if he didn't steal it? It is just so unfair. *He didn't come and have lunch with Pip and me and when we went to find him he was sitting under a tree looking all pale and he wouldn't tell us what had happened for ages. I think he had been crying. Me and Pip tried to cheer him up but how can he be happy about being labelled a thief when he is innocent? I am so furious. I wanted to go over to his house tonight but I have to stay home and look after Harry. Mum and Dad have gone to a movie. Things are weird around here. Since Mum went to the therapist she is acting very nicey-pie and she and Dad are being sickeningly lovey-dovey all over the place. Will it last? Who knows? Who cares? And what'll I do now? Harry is hogging the computer. I played with him for a while but I am all doomed out. Nothing on TV and for once I have done all my homework. I've been leaning out my window and listening to the far-away traffic hum and the small sounds of the suburbs, where nothing in particular ever happens. I feel bored and restless and edgy. School, dinner, television, sleep. School, dinner, television, sleep. Is this all there is? I want more.*

MALVINA/THURSDAY NIGHT/IN THE BATH

Something is up with Asher. I know he is upset about Nigel going out with that stupid Fiona woman, but the postcard came on Tuesday and on Wednesday he seemed pretty okay, yet tonight he is acting really strangely. He's hardly said a word all evening. It's so unusual for him not to finish his dinner. He loves fried rice. Now he's holed-up in his room playing that sad blues song over and over again. Roger mentioned there's a nasty virus going around so maybe he's coming down with that. I hate it when he goes all moody like this. Just like his father. Bloody Nigel. I mean, Fiona

Barrington for goodness sake. She's so ditzy and cutesy and insubstantial, and what about those awful day-glo surfie-girl outfits she wears. How could he? Well, he has and he does, apparently. I guess he's doing better than I am in the romance stakes. One false alarm with a gay guy and one drunken Irishman who called me 'sexy' at the train station. How does one meet men in a new town? When Nigel and I were together I longed for my freedom and now what have I got in the way of a social life? A hot bath and big dressing gown and a good novel . . . oh well, it could be worse. God, though, pea-brained Fiona Barrington, how could he?

ASHER

i hate it here i hate it this stupid flat and that awful stink from the factory why did we ever come here why couldn't my stupid parents have sorted themselves out now dad has got someone else already i'm damned if i want her for a stepmother stupid twitty thing and mum just sits around drinking wine and looking all sorry for herself she tries to act cheerful but she doesn't fool me she's miserable just like i am why the hell did we have to come here i hate that bloody school how could that pompous prick accuse me of stealing i never did anything that old bitch saying i was lurking around just because i was the last one out of the room well someone has to be last one out and it doesn't mean you are a thief well i'm not a thief but what good does being a decent person do you i can't talk to mum about this it will really upset her things are bad enough already i hate this bloody place i hate that bloody school all i want to do is to get out of here

FRIDAY LUNCHTIME/THE OVAL

Hi, Asher.

Hey, Rosie. Where's Pip?

She's away today. She's got the dreaded lurgy, well, a stomach ache actually. What did you have this morning?

Biology, which was boring, and then Double Art. We drew shells and stuff. What about you?

Ancient History and Maths. Then we played basketball in Phys Ed. I'm pooped. What have you got for lunch, Ash?

Leftover fried rice. It tastes better than it looks. Want some?

Nah, I'll stick with my yoghurt, thanks. I've got an orange somewhere as well.

What did you do last night?

Nothing much. My oldies went out. I was supposed to be babysitting my little brother but he doesn't need looking after. He just hangs out in front of the computer. It was a boring night. Umm, actually . . . I was going to phone you but I don't have your number.

Give us something to write it on then.

Put it on my folder.

Give it here. So, what's yours?

Here, I'll write it on your arm.

Only thing is, Rosie . . .

What?

Nah, doesn't matter.

Asher, what?

Nothing.

What?

You can't tell anyone, not even Pip.

I won't. What is it?

I might not be there if you ring. I'm thinking of taking off again.

Oh, Asher. Why?

I hate it here. And get this. In Maths this morning a kid whispered at me, 'So what did you spend the money on, loser?'

Which kid?

I don't know. Some little blond twerp, I think. It was someone sitting behind me. I didn't see who it was. But I heard it.

Asher, that's totally unfair. We have to tell someone.

Tell who? McKenna? What good will that do? He thinks I did it. He can't stop a rumour anyway. Besides, who gives a toss? I just want to get out of here.

Did you talk to your mother about it last night?

Nah, no way.

Maybe you should.

What good will that do? Only freak her out.

I don't know. Are you really going to take off again?

Yeah, probably, but not to Byron. My dad can't have me there. I'm going to head up the coast, to Broome or somewhere. I just want to get out of here for a while. I don't really care where I go.

Asher.

What?

I want to come with you.

SOME IDEAS are not born of logic and good sense. They are made of clouds and cobwebs. They sprout from nowhere and feed on excitement, sprinkled with adventure-juice and the sweet flavour of the forbidden. The psyche moves from the realms of the ordinary and takes a delicate step towards the territory of the unknown. We know that we shouldn't and that is exactly why we do.

LETTER FROM NIGEL THAT ASHER NEVER GOT

Dear Asher,

I've been thinking of you a lot since we talked on the phone and hoping that things have settled down for you. I know it must be bloody hard taking on a new place and *a new school, and also getting the hang of living in a city after good old Byron. I wish it could be some other way. The next few months are going to be flat out for me. I'm flying up to Darwin on Tuesday to look at a site. The client, who is loaded with dosh, wants me to design a very fancy house-cum-art gallery with a Japanese feel, and also have some input into the landscaping of the garden as well, or the 'entire concept' as he keeps saying. It's a big job and I could do with the money. After that it will probably be at least six weeks at the drawing board, head down and bum up, to get the guts of it onto paper, with the odd trip back to Darwin to consult. And after that I will hop on another plane to come and see you.*

I miss you very much. Life feels pretty weird without you guys. I had one disastrous attempt at dating which I will tell you about sometime. For now, it is just me and the odd dip in the waves and far too much takeaway pizza.

All my love, Dad.

☎ FRIDAY AFTERNOON/3.30pm/ PHONE CALL ONE

Ash, it's me, Mum. What are you up to?

I just got in the door.

Oh, right. Look, a few people from the shop are going out after work for drinks and a meal and I thought I might go. How are you with that?

Fine with me.

Okay. Look, there's eggs in the fridge, heaps of salad stuff, cheese on toast, whatever. You sure you don't mind, Ash?

I don't mind.

Great, 'cause I need this one. It's been *such* a crummy week.

Sure, Mum. See you later, okay?

I don't know what time I'll be back, though. We might rock on to a movie.

Yeah, no worries. Bye, Mum.

Ciao, darling.

☎ FRIDAY AFTERNOON/3.35pm/ PHONE CALL TWO

Hello.

Rosie? It's Asher.

Hi.

My mum just called from work. She's going out tonight. If

you come over now we can get it happening. Do you still want to?

Yes.

Are you sure?

Yes.

Are you sure sure?

Yes.

Are you sure sure sure?

Asher, I told you. I'm sure. I want to come.

Bring the stuff then. If you're sure.

I'll be there as soon as I can. Asher? You do want me to, don't you?

Look, Rosie. I told you already. It's not that I don't want you to. It's just that I don't reckon you know what you're getting yourself into.

But do you want me to?

Yeah, I do.

I'll be there soon then. Bye.

NEXT

Rosie goes into the kitchen. Lily is distracted. She can't find where she left her cheque book and she has a horrible feeling that she left it on the counter of a giftware shop several hours earlier when she was buying that gorgeous mermaid tray. Rosie asks if she can stay the night with Pip and Lily thinks — with the half of her brain that is operating in the here and now — that actually it would be quite convenient if Rosie did stay at Pip's tonight because Harry is staying the night with a friend, and if Lily hurries she can drop him off on her way to the giftware shop and then she could go and meet Robert for a meal. Friday nights used to be like that before she had the kids, sitting on the balcony at the Brass Monkey, drinking a glass of champagne and taking their time deciding which restaurant to go to. If she rings Robert now it might just work out, and they could try that new Thai place everyone's raving about. So she says that Rosie can go if she can get over there on her bike and asks when she will be home and Rosie says that she and Pip might go to the markets in the morning but she'll be home in the afternoon about four o'clock and Lily thinks fair enough and calls Robert and grabs her car keys and her handbag and her son and gives Rosie a quick hug and dashes out the door.

SHE PACKS:

undies & socks & journal & pen
satin skirt & velvet bodice
rainbow dress & blue muslin dress
shampoo soap toothbrush hairbrush towel
bathers & sarong
ragged Bali shorts
old lace top
sleeping bag
3 pairs sparkly earrings
keycard
and then she puts on her black jeans and her white t-shirt and her black jacket and her Docs and before she can chicken out

she hugs Beethoven near to death and she hops on her bike and cycles flat out to Asher's house, stopping at Nightingale's pharmacy to buy a packet of Clairol Sunshine Blonde.

From LIVING WITH TEENAGERS

'EXPERIMENTATION IS A MAJOR ISSUE IN THE DEVELOPMENT OF A HEALTHY TEENAGER. THIS CAN MEAN A SEEMINGLY RECKLESS ABILITY TO TAKE RISKS WITH THEIR HEALTH AND SAFETY, SECURITY, PARENTAL ACCEPTANCE AND LOVE. THIS IS ALSO A TIME WHEN FANTASY AND IMAGINATION ARE STRONGLY IN PLAY AS THE INDIVIDUAL MOVES TOWARDS THE FUTURE AND BEHAVIOURS WHICH MAY RESULT ARE DAYDREAMING, UNREALISTIC AMBITIONS AND EXPLORING DIFFERENT REALITIES.'

HE PACKS:

undies & socks & toothbrush
grey trousers
Marilyn Monroe t-shirt
black jumper
paisley Indian shirt
green corduroy shorts
black beanie
sleeping bag
tent
two plastic bowls and two tin plates
one battered billy without a lid
two knives and two forks and two spoons

a packet of nuts and raisins

Swiss army knife

☎ 6.45pm/PHONE CALL TO PIP

Unrecorded

7pm/BUS STATION/PERTH

Two teenagers with really short blond hair get on a bus to Geraldton.

STRANGE SIGNS THEY SAW ON THE WAY

Mount Pet Supplies. For all your animal needs.

Janine. Happy 40th. Marry me, doll baby.

Danger. Tortoise Crossing.

Tomatoes for Sale. If you take my produce and don't leave any money I hope you choke on it.

Fish and Chips Hamburgers Crabs Legs Open

ROSIE ON THE BUS

This is crazy but I don't care. Mum and Dad won't even realise I'm gone until tomorrow afternoon. I'm not going to think about that now. My hair feels great, so light and fluffy. I can see my reflection in the window and I like the way I look. I look older too, seventeen maybe. I keep wanting to rub my hands through my hair and feel how it is, all neat and scrubby. But it does smell a bit odd. God, this is so weird. I hope Pip does what I asked her to and points the oldies in the wrong direction. Well, I have to admit it was a relief to take my nose-ring out. It was so uncomfortable when I blew my nose. No one will recognise us now. He smells funny, too, the chemical pong of the hair dye and a nice, musty, sweaty smell. Gee, I'm tired. I wonder where we'll sleep tonight? I want to be close to him. I think I might sort of lean against him.

ASHER ON THE BUS

what are you doing man it's one thing taking off by yourself but now she's here it's different more serious the thing of it is we've done it now and let's face it i don't want to turn back live in the moment tomorrow will take care of itself it feels good it's a real adventure the hair thing was a great idea of hers it's pretty amazing that she would go through with it her life has been very straight what dab hands with the scissors we turned out to be and hiding the dye packet and the plastic bag full of hair in a rubbish bin down the street was a stroke of brilliance i don't miss my dreads they were getting kind of itchy i wonder what this geraldton place is like and what are we going to do when we get off the bus i wonder what she's thinking maybe she's asleep . . . oh . . . is she . . . yes . . . she is . . . yeah . . . she's snuggling into me . . . what if i just put my arm around her very very gently

MALVINA/MIDNIGHT

She fumbles in her handbag, her long fingers seeking out the spiky edges of her new key ring. Malvina is very fond of her new key ring. It's a huge red plastic hibiscus, for which she paid $1.99 in a hardware store. A great find. Today she invoiced and despatched a huge order of art books and rearranged the entire Personal Growth section and now she is bone weary. It's a good sort of tired though. Her belly is comfortably full of linguine marinara and Greek salad washed down with a fruity dry white, followed by lemon tart with double cream. It was a shame that they didn't get to a movie but coffee at Roger's place had been good — slow jazz and lazy conversation. Thank goodness for Friday nights. Two whole days of freedom and a decent sleep-in tomorrow. Malvina opens the door. The flat is quiet and calm, the morning paper still spread out on the table, Asher's schoolbag thrown down beside the couch, her big arrangement of ragged-petalled chrysanthemums welcoming her with their bright flash of pink. Oh, how flowers lift the spirits, she thinks sleepily. Sometimes Malvina goes in to give her sleeping son a kiss, or pull up his doona but tonight his door is closed and she is exhausted. Thank heavens for Fridays, she thinks again, and hops into bed.

GERALDTON/MIDNIGHT/THE SEABREEZE GUEST HOUSE

Mrs Croft is wearing pink fluffy slippers and a rather grubby peachy-pink track suit. Her nicotine-stained fingers are gnarled but her nails are painted a lovely shade of cyclamen to show off her collection of marcasite rings. Her last perm wasn't the best one she's ever had and her patchy white hair sits on her head like a row of worried little sausages.

It's been a bad week for Ethel Croft. The ancient telly finally quit for good and she's had hardly any casual guests. On top of all that, Doug, one of her permanents, left to go and live with his daughter in Balga without giving two weeks' notice like he should have. How the hell is an old bird supposed to make a quid?

It's midnight and Ethel is still up. She's been sitting at the laminex table in the kitchen drinking port and lemonade, and playing patience with her old pack of cards that have pictures of greyhounds on them. So, when the night bell rings and she answers it and these two tired-looking young ones ask the price of a room, Ethel doesn't bother to ask any questions. She just takes their $25 and shows them the room and where the bathrooms are and shuffles off to bed.

THE ROOM

An ancient wooden wardrobe complete with two bent wire coat-hangers.
A dressing table with a plastic lace doiley strategically covering a huge burn mark.
A wooden bedside table with a bible in one drawer and a dead fly in the other.
One Bells Scotch Whisky ash tray.
A broken pink bedside lamp.
A double bed with a pink chenille bedspread.
The fusty smell of old carpet and strangers.

THE FIRST NIGHT

Down the one-bulb hall Rosie comes from the shower, wearing her t-shirt and her sarong. She is so tired she is stumbling. She is shy. She is scared. But she's still glad she's there. Asher is already in bed, lying on his back with his brown arms behind his head, his hair damp from the shower. He winks at her. Her smile lights up the night. Rosie turns off the light, takes off her sarong, and hops in. Slowly, tenderly, like an old married couple, they tuck in together like spoons and to the sounds of a drunken fight outside on the street they fall asleep, awash with happiness.

DREAMING

She dreams she is in a supermarket, a dazzling three-ring circus of a place that smells of fresh bread and roasted nuts. There are sequined light bulbs, magnificent towers of glittering cans, packets galore of unimaginable delights, minarets of glistening ruby red plums and sweet oranges. She is not in the least bit surprised to see that the woman behind the deli counter is Lily. Dressed in ice blue, with a snazzy bow in her hair, her mother is whispering softly, 'Chocolate is bad for you.'

He dreams he is bicycling through the night sky, wild and long-legged and joyous. Over the tops of the terrace houses he pedals happily, far above the blue-tiled roof-tops, the glow of starry white geraniums in a window box, and a marmalade cat sliding through velvet blackness. His shirt flaps ragged in the night air. He is yelling with happiness, wildly, like a tribesman.

And then, suddenly, Oh darn, he thinks, blushing. Where on earth are my trousers?

THE FIRST MORNING

They wake late and it is sweet to lie in each other's arms pretending to be asleep because it feels so good and if you said anything it might break the spell. Then Asher looks at his watch and wow, it's nine-thirty already so they climb out of bed and pull on their clothes and pad bare-footed along the musty corridor to the bathroom, where they splash their faces awake with brown cold water from the rusty pipes. They check out the empty guest lounge, which is home to a family of geriatric armchairs, a vase of plastic gladioli, a pile of tattered *Who* magazines and a painting of a lurid sunset. Beside that is a small, smelly alcove with a kettle and the fixings for drinks. How neat to discover that they both take coffee the same way, white with two sugars. How companionable to drink it together, sitting in wobbly cane chairs on the verandah overlooking the back of a Chinese restaurant. Asher says, 'Man, I am starving,' and Rosie says, 'Me too,' and so they pack their stuff and leave the key in the bedroom door and set off to find themselves some breakfast.

BREAKFAST

Four fresh buttery croissants in a white paper bag from the Mainstreet Bakery, two crunchy apples and a shared orange juice, consumed on the beach, surrounded by sixteen seagulls. How come there is always a gull with only one leg?

ROSIE'S KEYCARD SLIP

$189.42

ASHER'S KEYCARD SLIP

$51.93

MALVINA/10am/SATURDAY MORNING

Lazily she stretches and looks out the window to find wide sky and soft sunlight. Another day in paradise. Okay, so the summer had been hot enough to fry a cat but now, with autumn putting a toe around the corner, each gorgeous clear day was a delight. In New Zealand it would be cold and rainy by now. Shall I get up, Malvina wonders idly. Why don't I just make myself a pot of Earl Grey and some raisin toast and hop back into bed and read *The Shipping News*. Doesn't sound like Ash is up and about yet, so why the hell not? I can go to the markets for veggies this afternoon and the rest of the chores can wait until the cows come home for all I care.

PIP'S HOUSE/11am/SATURDAY MORNING

Mum, can I go to town today?

How come, love?

Me and Sara and Lucy are going to the pictures, and Lucy's going to buy some shoes, too.

What about your homework?

I've hardly got any. Just a take-home test for Biology. I'll do it tomorrow, no worries.

Well, okay. Sort out your washing first though.

I did already.

So when will you be home?

Five-thirty?

Yes, that should be all right. Your dad's working all day and even if I go over to Maggie's I'll be back by then. We'll get a pizza for tea.

Yumbo. Can I have my pocket money?

Bring me my bag then, hon. It's in the bedroom. How come Rosie isn't going?

Um . . . she's doing something with her parents today.

Here, you're in luck, 'cause I've got the right change. Don't spend it all in one shop.

Thanks, Mum. See you later.

GROOVING IN GERALDTON/ SATURDAY/1pm

Their bags are heavy so they spend a buck and put them in a locker at the bus station and then they go exploring. Four op shops later Asher is wearing baggy olive cords, a white shirt with mother-of-pearl buttons and a pair of snazzy green tartan socks. Rosie carries her two treasures in a plastic bag: a blue silk rose-patterned scarf and a soft lavender batik sarong that only has one little hole in it. It was fun, trying on big furry coats and witty hats and laughing a lot.

Now they are mucking around in the park by the waterfront, sculling water from the fountain and playing on the swings. Rosie is hungry again but she's too shy to say so and Asher is hungry too but he's worried about money so he doesn't say anything either. Finally the smell from the fish and chip shop tantalises them so much that they get two bucks worth of chips and eat most of them and feed the last cold greasy crumbs to the gulls. How come the one-legged gull is always the pushiest?

MALVINA / SATURDAY / 1pm

Engrossed in the story of Quoyle in wild and stormy Newfoundland, Malvina reads on and on but finally her body says it is ready to get up and moving, especially as the sheets somehow feel a bit gritty and toast-crumby, although she may be imagining it. It could be the idea of it, just as you always feel itchy when you think about fleas. Either way it is well and truly time to get up and fling herself into Saturday, Malvina decides, so up she gets and has a long, hot shower.

She puts on her joyful outfit — baggy cream hemp vest and trousers and bright sunflower earrings — and sits in the sun to dry her hair. That's funny, she thinks. There is a girl's bike, a red one, parked beside Asher's black one on the back porch. And where on earth is Asher, anyway? Odd that he hasn't surfaced yet. Perhaps he did get up, though, and has gone off somewhere. A vague uneasy feeling nags at her subconscious so she looks in his room, but he isn't there, just a curtain blowing in the breeze, the rumpled black doona, the wooden guitar. He must have got up ages ago . . . Ah, I know, I bet that girl came over, Rosie, on her bike, earlier, while I was asleep, and they've gone off to the markets or somewhere. Funny he hasn't left me a note, though, but he doesn't always. I guess they'll be back soon.

Malvina wanders into the kitchen and bites into a juicy plum. Where shall I start with this mess, she wonders. The vacuuming? Bung a load of washing in? Blow it, she decides. I'd rather have a coffee at Gino's. Then I'll stroll up to the markets and buy the vegies. Mushrooms, she thinks, a big shiny eggplant, a slender zucchini or two. We'll have ratatouille for dinner, with rice, and grated cheese all melting and yummy sprinkled on top. By the time I get back Asher and Rosie will have shown up. Maybe Rosie would like to stay for dinner . . . maybe we could get out a funny video and the three of us could watch it . . . Monty Python, Cheech and Chong, something hilarious.

She feels empty and hopeful all at the same time, missing the not-so-long ago days when she and Nigel and Asher would spend Saturday nights together like that, comfortable, lazy, a family. I have to start filling the gaps, she thinks, flow with the changes, embrace the *now*. But somehow she still feels uneasy. There's no milky bowl in the sink, no cereal spilt on the bench, none of the usual signs of the Asher breakfast experience. She laughs. Maybe he's having an Egg McMuffin. It's a silly joke they share, whenever they run out of breakfast cereal one of them says, oh well, there's always an Egg McMuffin. Malvina has never seen or eaten an Egg McMuffin but it sounds wonderfully silly and every time they say it it sounds sillier and sillier. For some reason it makes her visualise a chubby cartoon figure wearing a beret and a tartan scarf; a ridiculous fellow, a buffoon. Just call me Egg, Egg McMuffin. Gradually her mind floats back to here, now, Fremantle, in the kitchen, Saturday morning, and the whereabouts of her son. Maybe he just grabbed an apple and went off with the girl. She'll leave him a note, a note, yes, that's what she'll do, and go and have that coffee. A cappuccino, hot and frothy, and sit in the sun and read the paper, and try not to think about Nigel.

✉ SHE LEAVES A NOTE/IT SAYS

Asher, not sure where you are but I'm off to do some shopping and stuff. See you later. Rosie can stay for tea if she wants.

Love Mum x

SATURDAY/AFTER LUNCH/ THE MOONS' HOUSE

Harry, are you going to finish that apple or not?

I have finished it.

Hand it over here, lad. There's still heaps left on it. So, what have you got planned for this afternoon, Lily?

Nothing, really. I half wondered if we might take Harry to see *Babe*. It's on at three o'clock at the Preston in Como.

Oh, please, Dad, that'd be cool, can we?

Well, yeah, why not. What time will Rosie be back from Pip's?

About four, she said. We can leave her a note though. She's got her key. We'd be back around half past five anyway.

What about dinner?

I thought Chinese takeaway or something.

Great. Let's do it. I wouldn't mind stopping on the way at that decent nursery in South Perth to buy some petunia seedlings for under the lemon tree.

Okay, well, let's go now then. If we're early we can have a walk on the foreshore. Harry, do your teeth and get your shoes on. I'll put this stuff in the dishwasher and then we'll go.

PLACES ROSIE AND ASHER THINK ABOUT SLEEPING

Another night at the Seabreeze Guest House

Tent site at caravan park

Hitch-hike out of town and camp in bush

The garden shed in the park

The Backpackers' Delight

CONSIDERATIONS

Money

Vibes

Not wanting to attract attention

Excitement rating

Novelty value

MUTUAL CHOICE

The bush camp

GERALDTON/3pm

So they went to the locker and retrieved their gear. They found a big Coke bottle, rinsed it out and filled it up with water, and then they bought a packet of Weetbix and a packet of muffins and a packet of tomato soup and a carton of milk and four oranges and a small jar of peanut butter and six chocolate frogs, and $13 lighter they hit the road. Hitting the road sounded easy but actually involved trudging for twenty-seven hot, boring minutes to get to the outskirts of the town. Thumbs out but nothing happened. The cars just rolled on by, dusty utes and white Holdens and a blue Mercedes, but no one stopped. So they started walking, silently, bothered by pesky flies and heavy shoes and cumbersome bags and hot feet, each lost in their own quiet thoughts.

ROSIE

How weird. Twenty-four hours and they don't even know I'm gone yet. Mum will go ape. Dad too, I guess. Maybe I should have left a note. Too bad, they'll figure it out. Maybe I could phone them next time we're in a town, just so they know that I'm all right. I wouldn't have to say where I am. Pip better not crack. Jeez, I'm sick of walking. Are we ever going to get a lift? Hope he doesn't think I'm too much of a dag, because I don't know toot about camping. I've never done any really. Our holidays have always been in cabins or hotels. I guess I'll manage . . . but what will we do for toilet paper? I hope I've got a tissue or two down at the bottom of my bag.

ASHER

this scrub is no good for putting the tent up too open no decent cover hope we get a long ride that takes us into a different sort of country this tent is pretty damn heavy wonder what she's thinking she's very quiet maybe she can't handle it maybe she won't like camping like mum she doesn't like roughing it much any more my hippie days are done ash is what she says give me a posh hotel and a hot shower any day but i love the bush dad does too the quiet and the trees and the sky i just wish someone would give us a goddam ride

WHAT THEY SHOULD HAVE REMEMBERED TO BRING

A box of matches

AT THE COMO

It's four o'clock, and here's Harry, wedged into a grey plush seat in the middle of the third row from the back. He's got a bucket of popcorn in one hand and a small cardboard cup of lemon fizz in the other. He's got Lily on one side and Robert on the other, and he's laughing his head off at the antics of a loveable talking piglet. This has got to be small boy heaven.

THE ROAD MOVIE CONTINUES/ 4.10pm

Ah, it's a great life if you don't weaken. John Diamond is a big man and he's had a big week fencing on his big sheep station just out of Meekatharra. Darn nuisance that he had to come all the way down to Geraldton just to get a part for the bloody tractor. Ah, well, good thing the pimply yobbo managed to order the right one in, although paying him $118.95 for the privilege had been a bit of a hard ask. Never mind, he'd got a few other errands done including picking up some special knitting wool for the wife. Bloody embarrassing that, going into the craft shop. The things a man has to do. Ah, but it had been good to have a beer and a feed at the pub. Seafood platter, just the ticket. Fancy Pat Reilly kicking the bucket. You never knew when your turn was coming, and that was for certain.

Anyway, he was headed home, and with a good run he'd be back just in time to crack a cold one and catch the sports and the weather report. Foot down hard on the pedal, a hairy brown arm out the window, greasy Akubra hat perched at a frisky angle on what's left of his ginger hair. John Diamond pops a tape into the tape deck. There's a choice of two: Patsy Cline and Jim Reeves Sing Your All Time Favourites, or the soundtrack of *The Big Chill*, which one of the jackaroos left behind once upon a time and which he plays every now and again just for a bit of variety. But for now, what could be better than a bit of good old country music to help pass the time, so hello Patsy, hello Jim, let's go walking after midnight. Now how about that, there's a couple of boys hitch-hiking up ahead. At least they're walking, giving it a bit of a go, not like some of these lean-against-a-tree-the-world-owes-me-a-living types. Might as well give them a ride, although God knows where they'd be off to this late in the day.

MALVINA/3.30pm

It's been a good afternoon. A lazy coffee in the sun, dipping into the Saturday paper and watching the world go by, and an hour of gentle cruising round the markets. There are two sorts of people, those who like shopping and those who don't, and Malvina is the first sort. Glittering jewellery from India, bright embroidered shoes, second-hand books, Balinese mobiles, little mountains of dates and strawberries — everything delights her. What a pleasure it is just to look, to daydream, to stroke and smell and touch. She wanders home past the boat harbour and the old houses, dreamily, contentedly. Unlocks the door, sees her note still propped against the biscuit tin. The little shit, she thinks, I'm going to blast him when he gets home. She can feel a good lecture coming on, a sensible one about responsibility and living in the city. Her morning anxiety is gone. Then, glancing out the window, she sees the two bikes still leaning against each other. It's such a lovely day and oh well, she guesses, Asher and Rosie are off enjoying themselves somewhere. Perhaps they went to the beach. Somehow she knows that by dinnertime Asher will be home, famished and apologetic. He'll smile that smile, the tiny quirky one that makes him look just like Nigel, and say he's sorry, Mum, and that he'll leave a note next time. I'm pooped, she thinks, plonking the grocery bags down on the bench. I'll just have a bit of a lie down and then I'll unpack all this stuff and start the dinner.

THE MOONS' HOUSE/5.30pm

Mum, can I watch TV?

Honestly, Harry, you just got in the door. No, you go and have a bath and put your pyjamas on. Go on, scoot. Maybe you can watch something after dinner.

Oh, okay . . .

I thought Rosie was going to be home by now?

Well, she's supposed to be. She said about four.

Are we supposed to pick her up or what?

No, she took her bike. Look, can you have a look in that drawer for the Golden Dragon takeaway menu? I'm going to put the kettle on and make a cup of tea. Then I'll give Pip's place a ring and see where she is. Actually perhaps you will have to pick her and her bike up. It's starting to get dark.

Here's the menu. What'll we have?

I don't know. How about the Kway Tao noodles and that chicken-and-vegetable thing, and maybe a prawn omelette and a large fried rice.

Sounds good to me. The big question is, have we got any ice-cream?

Oh, Bob, you're hopeless. But yes, as a matter of fact, there's still some butter pecan left. Do you want a cup of tea?

Sure do.

Let's have it on the patio then.

Right.

I'll ring the Hekes' in a minute. Rosie's probably on her way home by now anyway.

You want me to carry the tray?

No, I'm all right, love.

SETTING UP CAMP / 5.30pm

You okay?

Yeah, only just though.

It was a bit rough.

A bit rough? It was downright bizarre.

I didn't think guys like that existed in real life. He was straight out of a *Crocodile Dundee* movie.

Yeah, really.

It was funny that he thought you were a boy.

All that beer had damaged his eyesight, not to mention melted his brain cells. I'd rather he went on thinking I was a boy than keep calling me 'girlie' like he did.

You were great, Rosie, acting like you were going to spew like that.

Well, we had to get out somehow. Any darker and we wouldn't have been able to make a camp.

Speaking of which, give us a hand with this, will you? Just hold on to this bit while I put the pole through.

I wonder if he believed me?

He seemed to. Saying we were going to hitch back to Geraldton was a good touch.

I did something else rather brilliant, too.

What?

I nicked these matches.

Shit, matches, I forgot all about matches.

Yeah, I just saw them on the seat with all the other rubbish and bingo, into the pocket, just in case.

We'll have to go easy on the water though.

Mmm. If we each have a mug now and use some for the soup we can save the rest for the morning.

We'll have to move on in the morning for sure.

The thing is, Asher . . .

What?

Well, where exactly are we going?

Just up the coast. Kalbarri, Broome, that's what I thought we agreed on.

Yeah, but Asher . . .

What?

I think we're on the wrong road.

What do you mean?

Well, we came on holiday up this way once. Actually we went to Monkey Mia to see the dolphins. And I think we're on the wrong road. There's a coast one and an inland one and we want the coast one, but if he was headed for Meekatharra then we're on the inland one.

Shit.

But it doesn't matter really. I mean, we're in no hurry or anything. We can hitch back in the morning. Back to that roundabout, just out of Geraldton. That's where I think we blew it. We can get a map from a petrol station, too.

Yeah, I guess. Hey presto, home sweet home.

It's a cute tent.

My dad got it for me for Christmas — it's called a silver dome. Now what we need is some small sticks for kindling.

Bloomin' mossies. What we need is insect repellent and a nice foam mattress.

Will a chocolate frog do instead?

Yeah, well, make that three and an orange and you've got a deal.

CHAIN OF EVENTS

Hi, Vera, it's Lily here. Rosie's not home yet and we just wondered if Bob should come over and get her, bring her bike home on the bike rack, seeing it's getting a bit dark.

I'm sorry?

That's if she hasn't left yet?

I'm not with you. Rosie hasn't been here today.

What?

Pip's been in town with the other girls today. She said Rosie wasn't coming. Said she was doing something with you guys.

But . . . Rosie . . . Rosie's got to be with you. She said she was staying the night with Pip.

Staying with us tonight?

No, last night. She came home from school yesterday and asked if she could stay with Pip. She said they were going to the markets today and she'd be home about four. We've been out ourselves and we thought she'd be home any minute. Oh my God, something dreadful must have happened to her.

Look, I don't know anything about any of this. Don't you worry yet. I'll talk to Pippa and I'll ring you back in a minute.

Okay. Thank you. Bye.

PIP'S STORY

Pippa, come here. Where's Rosie?

I don't know.

Come on, girl. Don't give me that. Where's Rosie?

Isn't she at home?

Pippa. You know she isn't at home. Lily just rang. Rosie told her mum she was coming here last night and she still isn't home. Now, where is she?

How should I know?

Girl, I know you know something about this. That woman is going out of her mind right now. Thinks her kid is murdered or something. Now this morning when I said was Rosie going to town, I knew *then* you weren't telling me the whole story. You had that flaky look on your face. You know something about this and you're going to tell me what it is. No more bunkum.

Well, she's with Asher.

That new boy?

Yeah. This thing happened at school. They said he stole some money and he didn't. Just because he's new and he looks a bit feral. It's so unfair. Anyway, he said he was taking off and Rosie said she was going too.

Holy Christmas! So where are they?

I dunno. Adelaide, I think. They were going to hitch across the Nullarbor and go back to Byron Bay where Asher lived before his mum and dad split up.

Pip, is this dead set?

Yeah.

It better be, girl. You go and get your father. I want to tell him about this. I've got to ring Rosie's mum. Poor woman, this is going to spin her right out.

MALVINA / SATURDAY / 5.45pm

It's getting late and she's chopping zucchini and she knows something is badly wrong and she doesn't know what to do or who to call and her belly feels like ice and her heart feels like coal so she stops chopping and starts to cry and right then there's a knock on the door.

AT THE CAMP

The mosquitoes are having a banquet and Rosie and Asher are having tomato soup with muffins and the first star has just come twinkling out. Gum trees are etched like Art Deco ink drawings against the horizon and the last of the black crows has screeched off into the dusk. There's a sweet lonely contentment to it, just two young lovers and a tent, under a dark blue satin sky.

HOT ON THE WRONG TRAIL

Mrs Fielding?

Yes.

I'm Detective Marsden, and this is Constable Fraser. May we come in?

Of course.

Is your son Asher at home?

No, he isn't. Actually I was just about to ring you. I thought he was out with a friend and they haven't come home and I'm terribly worried.

This friend, would it be a girl called Rose Elizabeth Moon?

Rosie . . . Yes, I think so. She's the only girl Asher ever brought home . . . I haven't seen either of them today, but a girl's bike is here. What is it? What's going on?

Mrs Fielding, I'm here because Mr and Mrs Moon have reported their daughter missing. She said she was going to stay at a girlfriend's house last night and when she didn't return this evening the parents became alarmed. Pippa Heke, the friend, claims that Asher and Rosie ran away last night and are hitchhiking across the Nullarbor, on their way to Byron Bay. Now our records show this is not a first attempt for your son. The same thing happened a few weeks ago, did it not?

Well, yes, but Asher seemed fine now. I mean he seemed to have settled back into school and everything . . .

Well, there's more to it, apparently. Pippa says that Asher was under suspicion for stealing a teacher's wallet at school. Do you know anything about this?

No. No, I don't. But Asher has always been very trustworthy. He just wouldn't do something like that, I know it. Although I must admit that he did seem a bit upset about something a few days ago. Why on earth didn't he tell me about it? This is terrible.

Mrs Fielding, don't get alarmed. This must be very upsetting for you but what we need to do now is get those two safely home again. Can you tell me exactly what your son was wearing on Friday night when he left the house?

Friday night? He can't have been gone since then. Oh, God. I mean, I went out last night. I got home late and I just assumed Ash was in bed. This morning when I saw the bikes I thought he and Rosie had gone off somewhere. So I'm not sure what he was wearing. But I can look in his room.

Thank you, Mrs Fielding, that would be very helpful.

Malvina goes in to Asher's room. Her mind is running in ten thousand directions at once. This is serious, she thinks. Nigel, where are you now I need you so badly? They'll take Asher away from me. They'll think I can't control him. They'll put him in a boys' home. What if he has an accident? Why didn't he tell me about the wallet? What am I going to do with a huge pot of ratatouille? Why didn't we stay in Byron? Why on earth did we come to this bad-luck place? How the heck am I going to figure out what he was wearing?

SURPRISE

Most of Asher's clothes are spread out on the floor, and there, amongst the gypsy ragbag of old shirts, lies a folded piece of blue paper with Mum written on it — blown down by the night breeze from the desk where Asher had left it, propped up with his little crystal pyramid.

✉ FROM ASHER

Mum — stay cool. i just have to do this, okay. i promise to stay safe and look after rosie. we will come back in a few weeks.

xox love Asher

PS. I did not take the wallet

NEXT

1 Detective Marsden says if they don't turn up within twenty-four hours a Missing Persons Alert Category 4C will be activated. Stay in touch, he says and starts to stride off

into the night. Oh, and we'll need a recent photograph.

2 Malvina says wait a minute and asks if it would be possible for her to speak with Rosie's parents.

3 Detective Marsden scratches his head and thinks about it and says well he doesn't see why not.

4 Malvina is given the Moons' phone number and the two policemen head off to a disturbance at a liquor store at Scarborough Beach.

CLUMSILY, LIKE A ROBOT WOMAN

Malvina phones Nigel, gets an answer-phone message saying, 'This is Nigel's machine. He's not available right now. Please leave a message and Nigel will call you back within thirty days or even sooner if you send him a large amount of money.' At any other time this would have been funny but not right now.

☎ LONG DISTANCE ECHOING LONELY

Nigel, it's Mal. Asher has taken off again. This time it's more serious . . . there's someone else involved. Look, I really need to talk to you. Ring me, okay?

Next, heart in her mouth, Malvina dials the number that the police have given her. Robert answers. Well, he says, my wife is pretty upset right now, but yes, we would like to talk to you about this. Would it be possible to get together in the morning? Eleven o'clock? I don't have a car, says Malvina, wondering if she sounds as incoherent as she feels. We can come to your place, says Robert. Give me your address.

After she puts the phone down Malvina goes into the kitchen. There are the eggplant, the zucchini, the mushrooms, the chopping board, the knife. Despite everything she realises that she is hungry. She shoves the eggplant into the fruit bowl, puts the zucchini into the fridge, throws the mushrooms into a frying pan with a good dollop of butter and puts two bits of toast in the toaster. Then she rings Roger. Like a happy miracle he is home. Look, can you come over, she asks him. Bring some red wine and a big box of tissues. This is Major Crisis time. I need a friend. Sure, sweet pea, says Roger. This is Gorgeously Gay Saturday Night Samaritans at your service. I'm on my way. Merlot or Cabernet Sauvignon?

ROBERT AND LILY TRY TO MAKE IT THROUGH THE NIGHT

Let's try and think positive, Lily. Getting panicky won't help.

I'm not panicky, for goodness sake! I'm worried. There is a difference, you know.

Look, Rosie is a sensible girl . . .

Oh Robert, how can you say that? If she was so sensible she'd be home in bed!

I know you're upset, Lily. But we need to pull together on this one. Look, all teenagers go through a rebellious stage. The police know what they're doing. It's going to be okay.

I just hope to God you are right, that's all.

Let's get some sleep. It won't seem so bad in the morning.

THOUGHTS

And Robert thinks, Oh God, please let Rosie be safe. I musn't show Lily how terrified I am. I have to be strong. I have to be strong enough for both of us. I need a hug.

And Lily feels a hundred per cent alone and totally unable to reach out and she asks herself how come her husband is so unfeeling, how come he doesn't sound worried?

HARRY

Rosie's gone somewhere and Mum and Dad are all upset and they won't tell me about it properly. *Babe* was so cool. I liked the bit where she chased the sheep. I wish we went to the pictures every week. Rosie will come back soon. I know she will.

IN MALVINA'S GREEN SILK PHOTO BOX

Podgy baby Asher with a bald head, lying on a tartan rug, waving his little fat feet. Asher, two, in a funny old green cardigan and baggy trousers, clutching a plush monkey. Five, with his ears sticking out, proudly showing the cricket bat he got for Christmas. Eleven, all arms and legs, on the beach with Nigel and a Nat Young surfboard. Asher at the zoo. Asher in a sailor-suit. Asher in pyjamas. Asher in his tree-house. Asher and Nana and the giant pumpkin. School photographs. Asher and Jesse and Sam and Viv pretending to drive a wrecked Cadillac, full speed ahead and laughing. Asher, alone, playing his guitar on the back step. Malvina picks the most recent school photograph, close up, head and shoulders. Funny, she thinks. He isn't looking at the photographer. He's looking somewhere beyond.

KODAK ROSIE

The photograph Robert and Lily give to the police is the one that sits on Robert's desk, taken last summer by Harry when they were having a picnic down at the river. Most of Harry's shots are blurry headless numbers, which is why he hardly ever gets a turn at the camera, but this was the day that he kept hassling until Lily, made reckless by her second glass of champagne, gave in and said yes. Make sure you get the head, boy wonder, she had insisted, and so he did. There she is, Rosie, just her head and elegant neck, laughing, dark eyes and dark curls and the river smooth behind her. Picture perfect, all giggle and grin. It hurts to hand it over. If he hasn't got his daughter he wants to keep her photograph, but Robert does what has to be done. Here, he says, and walks across the room briskly. This is my daughter, Rosie.

TUCKED IN THEIR SLEEPING BAGS/ SATURDAY NIGHT

Rosie?

Mmm?

What are you thinking?

I was thinking about my parents. They'll know by now. They'll be pretty freaked.

How about you . . . are you freaked?

A bit.

Do you want to go back?

No, it's not that . . . it's just . . . they'll be incredibly worried, that's all.

You could ring them.

Yeah, I was thinking that. I will. In the morning when we go back to Geraldton. But I won't say where we are, let them keep thinking we're headed for the eastern states. I just don't want them to worry, that's all. I'll do what you did, tell them I'll be coming back in a few weeks.

How come you didn't want to leave them a note?

I don't know. I didn't know what to say, where to start. I just wanted to get out of there. I mean, the last few weeks have been better, hardly any arguments or anything. But before that, I don't know, it's been so awful. My mum and dad have been having a bad patch, they just don't seem to like each other much at all, well, maybe it's not that, but neither of them seem happy. My mother carries on and on about everything and my father clams up and that makes her carry on even more. Even when there's a good bit you're wondering when the next bad bit will be. And mum and me, we disagree about everything. It's like she doesn't want me to grow up, just wants me to do everything her way for ever. You name it, we fight about it. It just got to me. And so on Friday, all I could think about was getting away.

Yeah, I know. I felt like that too, just wanted to get away from it all, school, the wallet thing, and . . .

And what?

Nothing. Well . . . I'm glad you came too, that's all.

Asher?

What?

Have you had a lot of girlfriends?

No, only one, sort of.

Sort of?

There's this girl, Jesse, in Byron. The four of us, her and Viv and Sam and me, we got around together all the time. Same class at school, surfed together, everything. And me and Jesse were . . . I don't know, I guess you could say she was my girlfriend, but only sort of.

Like what?

Like . . . she was my friend and she was a girl and if I'd stayed in Byron I guess she would have been my girlfriend.

What does she look like?

Red hair, dreads, freckles. She wears stuff like you do.

Do you miss her?

I miss it all. I miss my father. I miss my friends. I miss my parents being together. How about you?

How about me what?

Have you had many boyfriends?

Nah, none. The odd crush, and there was this kid called Alex, his parents were friends of my parents and we got a bit interested in each other. He lived way out in Parkerville and he went to Eastern Hills High so I didn't actually see him very often. We used to talk on the phone a lot. But then he went all techno and started hanging out with these idiots . . . I went off him, I guess. Isn't it strange how people always ask if you've got A Girlfriend, capital letters, and try and put it in a box and nail it to the wall when it isn't really like that.

Tell me about it. My mother always asks me these revoltingly innocent, snoopy sort of questions about everything, ferreting away wanting to know stuff. For a while there she went on and on about Pip, like she thought we might be gay or something. I tell her as little as possible. Oh, yerk, there's that mossie again. I'm going to stick my head down into my bag to get away from it. I'm sleepy.

Yeah, me too. Sleep creepeth towards me through the sweet night, as my dad says.

Is that Shakespeare?

Nah, he made it up. He likes to make up stuff, pretend to be some famous poet. Calls himself Sir Nigel the Bard. He's bloody funny, too. Well, goodnight then.

Night night. I hope I don't tread on you.

What?

In the night. I hope I don't tread on you. I usually have to get up to wee.

Oh, right.

Goodnight then.

Yeah. Sweet dreams.

ROSIE/9pm

I wonder if he likes me more than he likes Jesse. I wonder how come he doesn't try to kiss me or anything. Blimey, I am *so* tired. Tomorrow I'll ring home. I might ring Pip too. I'll have to get a whole lot of coins. Or a phone card. Tomorrow we might kiss. Tomorrow we'll hitch to the sea. We need to buy a map and a toilet roll.

ASHER/9pm

this ground is hard not going to admit it though won't take long to fall asleep drifting already i really like being with her she is so easy to talk to i can say anything and it's all right i wish i had the nerve to kiss her how come it has to be the boy who does everything wish i was sophisticated and groovy not fifteen and terrified and i really wish that station-owner hadn't kept asking us where we were going to we kept sort of stalling him and changing the subject but he must have realised we were avoiding answering him properly go away you pesky mossie a man needs his sleep i love this sleepy drifty floaty time just before you drifty floaty

EARLY SUNDAY UNDER A GUM TREE

At five-thirty bird song starts; the crows are making a hell of a racket. By six o'clock the travellers are half awake. At six-thirty Rosie stumbles out for a piddle. By seven the sun is shining brightly on the tent, so they get up and sit around, feeling slightly dazed as you do when you've slept on hard ground a long way from anything familiar and you wake to remember that you are a fugitive from the law in a dusty field fifty kilometres from the nearest town. Seven-thirty and it's time to eat Weetbix drowned in milk and peel a juicy orange. At eight o'clock Asher and Rosie hear the whine of a trail bike somewhere a bit too close for comfort; this is, after all, some farmer's land. Time to take the tent down, roll it up, throw sand on the traces of the fire and get back on the road. Heading south with not a car in sight.

WISHING

Wish a car would come
Wish it was a silver Porsche
Wish it was a purple Rolls Royce
Wish it was a black Merc with a tape deck playing The Doors
Wish it was a pink Cadillac playing Chocolate Starfish
Wish it was a gold Mercedes playing old blues music
Wish I had a mobile phone
Wish I had a cup of coffee, white with two sugars
Wish I did too
Wish I had a toasted cheese and tomato sandwich
Wish I had a ham and cheese toasted sandwich, and a cup of hot chocolate
Wish I had a motorbike
Wish I had a hot shower and a big fluffy towel
Wish I had a house by the ocean
Wish I had sandshoes on
Wish I had a donkey to carry my pack
Wish I had wings
Wish a car would pick us up
Wish it was a silver Porsche

A RIDE AT LAST

Miriam Perkins is on her way to St Patrick's Sunday Service in Geraldton in her 1979 yellow Corolla. She's driving just below the speed limit, sedate as ever, humming along to a stirring hymn that is playing on the devotional program on Radio National, when she sees these two girls hitch-hiking. Miriam Perkins doesn't believe in picking up hitch-hikers. Male hitch-hikers could be dangerous and female hitch-hikers are doing something dangerous, as far as Miriam is concerned, but because it is two girls and it is Sunday and the Lord said that we should Love Thy Neighbour as Thyself, she decides to make an exception for these two wee lassies. Even though there is no other vehicle in sight, she carefully indicates and gently pulls the Corolla to a stop at the edge of the dusty road. She shifts the plate of cling-wrapped homemade apple slice from the front seat onto her knee and puts her tidy little head out the window. I can give you two a lift to Geraldton, she trills, as long as one of you can pop the morning tea on your lap.

BACK IN PARENTSVILLE

It's eleven o'clock and Malvina has tidied the flat to within an inch of its life. She has vacuumed, hidden all evidence of the red-wine extravaganza, artistically arranged the sofa pillows and shoved the assorted clutter higgledy-piggledy into the hall cupboard. She has a tea tray ready, with milk in a little jug and a plate of Tim Tams. Tidying up gives her something to do, and she wants the place to look normal. Not like the house of the mother of a bad influence, a thief, a maladjusted runaway boy.

She knows that Asher is none of these things, but how can she convince two middle-class Swanbourne parents whose daughter has disappeared? She remembers asking Asher what Rosie's parents were like and he said that he thought they were kind of straight.

Let's face it, things couldn't be much worse if they tried. Nigel hasn't rung back, she has a red-wine headache, or it might be a tension headache, but anyhow it's a killer and how ever hard she tries her flat still looks like a hippie place, only now it looks like a suspiciously tidy hippie place. And oh no, there goes the doorbell.

☏ PHONE BOX/SUNDAY MORNING

A Saturday night drunk has broken the window and ripped up half the pages of the phone book and there's a vague smell of old urine, but Rosie doesn't notice these things. While she puts her coins in the slot she watches Asher. He sits cross-legged in the park, his pack beside him. How slender he looks, and how gorgeous with his brown face and short blond hair going all curly now that his dreads have been cut off. Imagine that twitty old biddy thinking he was a girl. Classic, first Mr Akubra mistook me for a boy and now Mrs Off-To-Church mistakes Asher for a wee lassie. Grownups don't really see us, all they see is jeans and Docs and short hair and their imaginations do the rest. It's like we're on different planets. Stuff it, I don't care, Rosie thinks. I don't care about any of it, except me and Asher. And no matter how spare Mum goes, I'm not going back yet.

In the eye of her mind she is walking along a beach a long

way from anywhere, just her and Asher, and they have made a Robinson Crusoe camp to live in. The sand is white and she is wearing her purple sarong and . . . this sun-spangled daydream is rudely interrupted by a metallic pip pip pip in her ear and then Lily's voice, but not the real Lily. 'Hello, you have reached the home of the Moon family. We're not home right now but your call is important to us. If you wish to speak to Robert, Lily, Rosie or Harry, please leave your name and number after the tone and we will return your call as soon as possible.'

☎ THE MESSAGE

Mum, Dad, this is Rosie. Yeah, um, by now you know that me and Asher have taken off. I'm sorry I didn't leave you a note but you don't need to worry about me 'cause we're being really safe and sensible and we'll be back in a few weeks. I guess you won't understand this but I need . . . I just need time out. Um, and it isn't Asher's fault because I wanted to come. He's a really nice person and he didn't steal anything. So, well, a big hug for Harry and you two and well, bye for now, okay, see ya.

ROSIE MOON AND ASHER FIELDING ARE SITTING IN A PARK

Nine-thirty. A daydream morning. Geraldton is a ghost town. No one around but Rosie and Asher and a fluffy grey cat. All the world is still asleep or lying snugly in bed thinking about getting up, or sitting in a kitchen making a cup of tea and lazily spreading Vegemite on a slice of crisp toast. Time is a foreign land now, and life is an unknown quantity to decipher any way they can. There is nothing that they have to do and no place that they have to be and no one is telling them what to do. It is splendid and wonderful and as scary as hell.

TALKING

Did you do it?

Yeah.

And?

They weren't home so I just left a message on the answer-phone. Hurray for modern technology 'cause I was dreading my mother answering. She'd have gone ape and tried to make me come home. I feel better now. I mean, they won't be so worried. And then I rang Pip but her father answered the phone so I quickly hung up. Asher, I was thinking. I reckon we should get about a hundred bucks out of the bank, because there won't be any banks or ATMs in the little seaside places and we'll need money for camp sites and food and stuff.

Yeah, I guess so.

And we need a map and a toilet roll.

And more matches. There's lots of dead ones in that box and hardly any good ones.

So we've got to go down the main street and find an ATM and a deli and a service station and then walk all the way back to that roundabout.

That sounds exhaustipating. Why don't we lie down under that tree and rest for a while first?

Yeah, why not? The sunshine is making me sleepy.

SUNDAY MORNING

Tom Hyde is cleaning the cars. He always cleans the cars on Sunday mornings. It is a soothing suburban ritual. On Sunday mornings Wendy goes to her aquarobics class and he cleans the cars. He doesn't really understand why Wendy bothers with the aquarobics class because on her way home she always stops at the deli and buys gourmet goodies like camembert and pâté for lunch, lovely kilojoule-rich treats that surely cancel out any weight loss that might have occurred as she wobbled around in the water with the other middle-aged ladies. There's no way he'll mention it though because he likes having Sunday mornings to himself and he has no wish to jeopardise the gourmet lunches. He also likes her fubsy body just the way it is and wishes she wouldn't diet. It makes her incredibly cranky. This has been a bad week for Wendy, and thus for him. Full-on dieting, pre-menstrual tension, lots of marking and the lost wallet business. A nightmare week from hell.

Ah, it's nice out here in the sun. Tom empties the bucket of hot soapy water under the palm tree, wrings out his chamois cloth, winds up the hose. He has finished the outsides of both cars. Now to vacuum the interiors and then he'll brew a cup of coffee and see who's winning the rugby. As Tom Hyde manoeuvres the nozzle of the vacuum cleaner under the front seat of Wendy's Honda, his hand dislodges something wedged between the carpet and the door. It is a black wallet.

A BLUE VOLKSWAGEN KOMBI

Once upon a time her name was Patricia Louise Stanford, but not any more. Now her name is Star. Her name is Star and her hair is the colour of moonbeams rippled with streaks of day-glo blue, and on her bare brown ankle she wears a chain of tiny silver bells that make music when she walks. She isn't walking now though. She is sitting in the front seat of a blue Volkswagen kombi, feeling very spaced out and ragged. Yesterday afternoon in Freo, talking while they smoked weed with Cody and Annie, heading north at dawn had seemed a wild idea. But in reality it had been kind of a hassle. Instant coffee and stale muesli in the messy early-morning kitchen at Solomon Street; Leo stepping in the cat-shit; not being able to find her velvet hat. Cody and Annie had said to travel safely and come again any time but the vibes had seemed wrong, like maybe they had outstayed their welcome.

Leo was pissing her off too. Ever since the flat tyre at Gingin he had hardly said a word, and somehow it was meant to be up to her to keep Angel happy and occupied. Drawing endless pictures with crayons. Playing I Spy over and over again. Reading aloud from the battered fairy-story book. Let's face it, travelling with a four-year-old could be a real drag. And this landscape was pretty boring as well, the white line of the Brand highway stretching on and on. Just dry paddocks on either side and nothing much to see.

Thank goodness Angel had finally dropped off to sleep, curled up in the back with her satin sucky cloth wound around her podgy little fingers. Bloody men. Bloody Leo. Refusing to join in and lighten the vibes. Okay, so wasting energy being shitty with him wasn't very spiritual of her, she could see that. Osho said one must enter the reality of time and space, not grasping, not demanding that people behave in certain ways to meet your emptiness. It wouldn't hurt Leo to join in, though. Maybe she could try an affirmation. I am peace. Peace is all around me. Let go. Let go. Let go. Fair enough. Wish I didn't have to let go of my wonderful black velvet hat though, thinks Star.

THE BUMPER STICKERS ON THE BLUE VOLKSWAGEN KOMBI

The goddess is dancing

Greenpeace

Magic Happens

My other car is a goggomobile

Dunsborough Caravan Park

Visualise Whirled Peas

SUNSHINE AND ROSES

with rolled-up towels for pillows rosie and asher lie on their backs on the grass the sky is gently blue no clouds they take off their shoes so their feet can breathe they wriggle their toes and talk about when they were little and what's your middle name and what's your favourite food and what job would you most hate to do and what is the worst thing a parent can say to a kid and what's your favourite film and what's your favourite book and what shall we have for lunch and maybe we should get going in a while they do not kiss but they both want to instead their feet touch and so do their arms it is electric magic their tiny arm hairs tingling happily lying together the sun warming them watching sky through green-leafed gum branch close enough to hear each other breathe sweet togetherness this lazy lying down dance of love

LEO

Once upon a time his name was Marcus William Parker, but not any more. Now his name is Leo. His name is Leo and he chose it because Leo is his star sign, and as he is a freckled giant of a man with a huge mane of ginger ringlets he feels much more like a Leo — a lion man radiant with the energy of the sun — than he ever felt like a Marcus, which is surely the name of a shorter, paler, more ordinary sort of a being. Once upon a time he was a law student but now he is an organic man, a traveller and a seeker after infinite truth. His name is Leo and he is hungry and as he drives he is counting down the kilometres to Geraldton on the roadside markers, 65, 60, 55 . . . In about half an hour they'll be there. Good-oh. Then they can stop and stretch and eat. Maybe Star and Angel will cheer up after that.

It has been a scratchy sort of a trip so far but up ahead are wide open spaces, deserted beaches, campfires and starry nights. Leo is glad to be getting out of town. Somehow the Fremantle scene got to be a bit of a drag after a while, all that coffee-strip posturing and mobile-phone-yuppie bullshit. Fucking focaccia. He wouldn't care if he never saw a sun-dried tomato ever again.

QUESTIONS

What was the most amazing thing that happened when you were little?
What is your middle name?
What is your favourite food?
What job would you most hate to do?
What is the worst thing a parent can say to a kid?
What's your favourite film?
What's your favourite book?
What do you want for lunch?

ANSWERS FROM UNDER A TREE

When I was little I went to see Harry born. It took ages and at dawn he slid out, all red and perfect.
When I was little my father built me a three-level tree-house and we slept in it for two nights and ate food we pulled up in a basket with a pulley.

Don't laugh, okay? Elizabeth. I hate it. It's totally dull. I would rather have Kate or Gloria for a middle name.

Mine is Bodhi. Bodhi is the name of the tree that the Buddha got enlightened under. I like it but if I chose another one it would be Sam.

My favourite sweet thing is chocolate, any sort, except those bars of Dairy Milk with revolting gooey centres. Cherry Ripes are yummy and even better if you put them in the freezer for a while. Chocolate cheesecake and sticky date pudding are the best desserts. My favourite savoury thing is chicken curry.

Hot chips. Life on this planet could not exist without hot chips with salt and a bit of vinegar. Ordinary ones are better than wedges, but a good wedge is okay, too. For sweets . . . my mum's apricot walnut crumble with cream, for sure.

I could never be a dentist. Yuck. All that bad breath and looking up people's hairy noses.

Ambulance driver . . . gruesome. Or bank clerk . . . dreary. Or a hemorrhoid specialist!

Parents shouldn't say, 'I told you so.'

'When I was your age . . . '

I loved *The Joy Luck Club*.

Pulp Fiction.

Jane Eyre.

Lord of the Rings.

Chicken salad roll and Coffee Chill.

Chicken salad roll and chips and Coffee Chill.

MALVINA WRITING IN HER JOURNAL ON SUNDAY AFTERNOON

Sunshine here on the back step. Just me and a cup of ginger tea. Tired. Everything feels unreal. Meeting Lily and Robert went bet-

ter than I expected. They are nice people, worried out of their minds, like me. We all pretended that we were sensible adults and said sensible things. Teenage rebellion. Let's not panic. Think positive. We compared stories, went over the facts, agreed to keep in touch. As Lily left her hands were shaking and Robert put his big hand on her shoulder to comfort her. At least they have each other. I feel more alone than the last flower in a field, as useless as a bald man's hairbrush, as confident as a snowflake in hell. Yet in my depths I understand Asher. I ran away once. I remember what it's like to be fifteen, to feel as though the deck is stacked against you, to long for escape. What I don't know is how to be a parent. All I can do is sit here in the sun and wait, sending out my small prayers of hope and safety.

THE BLUESMOBILE

Star and Angel and Leo are feeling cheerful again. They rolled in to Geraldton around noon, parked the Bluesmobile down by the water and tumbled out, glad to be on the road again. There's nothing like a beach to lift the spirits: clouds and winging gulls and turquoise blue to dazzle the eyes, cool sand between the toes, a creamy petticoat-hem of waves to dance in. Star did some yoga, a rippling series of Salutes to the Sun, stretching and bending and bowing and curving her body, loosening her car-morning kinks. Leo ran up the beach and when he was utterly knackered he turned around and strolled back again, bringing a delicate purple shell to put on the sandcastle that Angel was making near the water's edge. Soon they were all at it; Leo mounding up great rooms and walls and a wide moat all around, Star placing neat rows of white shells for windows, Angel scurrying off to find treasures to decorate the roof: a wisp of pink seaweed, a skerrick of smooth glass, an icy-pole stick for a flag pole. What a splendid castle, and as they worked they sang a long silly song about a hole in a bucket.

It's a very excellent sandcastle, isn't it? asked Angel.
Yes, very excellent, said Leo.
And a wicked princess lives there all by herself, said Angel.
Does she? asked Star.
Yes, said Angel. And her name is Murglemurtle. And she's hungry.
So am I, said Leo.
We've got pita bread, said Star. And peanut butter and raisins and sprouts.
Good-oh. I'll boil the billy, said Leo.

So they ate their lunch, sitting on an old blue paisley table-cloth. There were no crusts for the seagulls but there were apple cores which the birds greeted with wild ungrateful squawking. Angel dug holes in the sand and watched them fill up with seawater while her mother and father snoozed in the sun, and then they all hopped back in the kombi van and headed north again. They were about a mile out of town and Star was deep in the *Travellers Atlas of Western Australia*, trying to work out how far it was to Kalbarri, when Leo pulled over.
What's up? asked Star.
Couple of kids hitch-hiking. They look pretty groovy. Might as well give them a ride.

THOUSANDS OF MILES AWAY/ SUNDAY AFTERNOON

Nigel Fielding is driving home, only it doesn't feel like home any more. Since Malvina and Asher left, the house feels like a series of empty rooms and a fridge with bugger all in it. Which is why he has been making an effort to get out, do things, see people, just as everyone keeps telling him to. But this weekend has been an absolute disaster. Everyone in Byron seems to think that he is having a steamy love affair with Fiona Barrington, but everyone in Byron is wrong. Actually he and Fiona have only seen each other three times and each time has been more awful than the last. First a cup of coffee and a movie. She had surprised him by inviting him out and it had been pleasant enough, although seeing *Muriel's Wedding* was a bit of a mistake, since one of the themes was family break-ups; gritty territory for both of them. Next, the party at the tennis club, where he had felt like an idiot trying to remember how to dance in public and had drunk too much tequila.

But last night, the third time, had been a total disaster. He'd gone to Fiona's house for dinner and somehow he'd ended up staying the night, more because it had seemed to be expected of him than because he'd really wanted to. After they had tentatively tucked into bed, Fiona had told him she was looking for a 'serious relationship' and he had suddenly realised with gut-wrenching clarity that what he really wanted was someone who would listen to him talk about Malvina, and that all he had in common with this lost fairy-like woman whose bed he was in was that they were both as lonely as hell. So he had done an 'I'm not ready for commitment' speech which had come out sounding as weak as water. Then they had kissed sadly and fallen asleep.

This morning, over croissants and coffee, there had been great awkward gaps in the conversation and when they said, 'See you soon' they had both known that the only seeing they might do was accidentally in the grocery store. Thank goodness he had to go to Darwin on Tuesday. Getting away would be a relief. So much for his foray into the wonderful world of dating. Let's face it, he admits wistfully, I miss Malvina and Asher like mad, and nothing can fill the gap.

Nigel parks his blue station-wagon under the jacaranda tree, grabs his mail, which consists of one lonesome telephone bill, and goes inside to be greeted by a very hungry cat and a flashing red light on his answer-phone.

FEELING GROOVY

This is the life, thinks Rosie. She and Asher are in the back of the blue kombi rolling along towards Kalbarri. A ride all the way. Yes. Yes. Yes. While waiting hot and sweaty by the side of the road it had seemed they were destined to never get any further than Geraldton. Praise be to the eternal law of impermanence. One minute cranky and down-hearted, the next minute rolling along on their way to the exact place they wanted to go.

She remembers Kalbarri vaguely from a long-ago holiday. She recalls a small windy place, blue sea, red rocks, low scrub, a sprinkling of shops and houses. Maybe they could pitch their tent in the caravan park and she could have a hot shower. I am beginning to pong, thinks Rosie. I love this van. It has to be one of the nicest places ever, a whole little travelling world. There is a table and two benches that become beds at night, and a little gas stove and sink, and a shelf with a neat row of jars full of noodles and beans and raisins and nuts. There are dolphin stickers and bright mandalas on the windows, and from the ceiling hangs a mobile made of green glass beads and gumnuts and shells. There are books and tapes and snorkels and towels all tucked neatly under the benches. There are story books and teddy bears and rainbow paper and crayons and jigsaws tucked into a box decorated with angels, and a small rolled-up foam mattress and a bright patchwork quilt and a pink star-spangled pillow to go on it. Rosie feels rescued and safe, part of something that tastes good. The curtains even have red roses on them. I am Rosie. I am roses. I am a gypsy traveller. I am an adventurer. I need a shower. I love Asher. There he is. His beautiful eyes. His thin brown hands. He winks at me. And I wink back. It didn't even feel like a squashy one.

ANGEL

The little girl stares at Rosie and Asher, quietly, thumb in mouth, round-eyed, watching.

ASHER

kalbarri good never been there but rosie has a fishing town she said with amazing rocks nearby these people are byron bay people classic hippies in the blue vw microbus they remind me of rick and squizzy who used to live in rainbowland with mum and dad cool that they gave us a ride even better that they haven't asked us any questions the little kid is cute like a fat pixie wonder what her name is she sure likes to stare though now the guy is putting a tape in dylan desire cool miss my tapes rosie looks beautiful even with her funny short hair when she smiles i feel it in my toes now she's staring at me i wink and she tries to wink back cute her nose all squashy wonder how long it will be till we get there i am a bit peckish do we have any chocolate frogs left no damn we ate them all i could go a bowl of pesto pasta with melted cheese

INTERROGATION BY ANGEL

What's your name?

Rosie.

Oh. What's his name?

That's Ash.

Cigarette Ash?

No, not cigarette ash. His name is Asher, but sometimes he gets called Ash. Nothing to do with cigarettes. What's your name?

Murglemurtle.

Murglemurtle?

It isn't really. I'm Angel.

Angel?

Yeah. It is really. How old are you?

Fifteen.

Oh. How old is he?

Fifteen. How old are you?

Fifteen.

Um, I don't think you're really fifteen.

How come?

Because you are quite little. Fifteen is big like us.

Well, I'm quite big for four, Star said so.

Star?

My mummy. Star. In the front.

Oh.

Leo's my daddy and Star is my mummy. Where's your mummy?

In Perth.

Oh. What's she doing?

Ah, I don't know really. She might be . . . she might be watching TV.

TV is crap. Leo said so.

Oh.

But I like it. I like cartoons.

Which ones do you like?

I like horsey ones and fairy ones and not silly ones with killing. Do you like those ones?

Yes.

Oh. I do too.

LATE AFTERNOON/NEAR KALBARRI/ FRONT SEAT

Well, nearly there.

Mmmm. We need to get milk and bread. We can ask at the shop about camping in the National Park. And if we can find one I wouldn't mind a decent cup of coffee.

Me, too. What about these kids?

What do you mean, what about them?

Are they runaways, do you reckon?

They could be. They're very young.

Should we just drop them off in town?

Angel seems to like them. I do too. They've got a nice feel about them.

I guess they could camp with us for a night, although if they're wanted by the cops we could be buying into a whole heap of trouble.

One night wouldn't hurt. They seem kind of lost.

Stray kittens and lost souls . . . your specialty.

Oh, Leo. You're a soft-hearted bear yourself. They might not want to anyway. Maybe they've come up here to stay with relatives or something.

Nah. There's a feral feel about them. Let's check it out.

Hey, you guys. We're going out to Bluff Knoll to set up camp for the night. You want to come along?

Um . . . actually we'd love to, wouldn't we, Rosie?

Yeah, that would be great. That is if you don't mind.

Nah, the more the merrier. Come on, let's go and see if we can find a cappuccino in this here little town.

FEELING GUILTY

Pippa Heke is sprawled in front of the TV watching *The Nanny*. She is wearing her sixties purple chenille cardigan and her baggy pink corduroy jeans and she is steadily working her way through a large packet of Mrs Murphy's Salt and Vinegar Crisps. It is making her thirsty. In the kitchen her mother is banging the pots loudly as she cooks, Vera's favourite way of letting Pippa know that she, Pippa, is in deep trouble. Ever since the phone call that morning Vera hasn't let up.

Crash. Dong. Whump. I know there's something you're not telling me, girl. Smash. Bang. Clunk. These kids could be in quite a lot of danger, so you better be giving it to me straight, Pippa Heke. Thump. Whack. Clang. Those poor parents. What a terrible thing. If they haven't been given the full story there'll be a whole lot of trouble, that's for sure. Clatter. Whack. Bump. Crash. Whump. Bang.

Pippa is beginning to think that what her big sister, Ruby, used to tell her must be true, that when you tell a lie it is Written In Big Green Letters All Over Your Forehead. How come her mother always knew when she was lying? It was as if she had a solid gold bullshit detector that never failed. Look, last time Asher took off he had headed across the Nullarbor for Byron Bay, right? So him and Rosie going there again made perfect sense, didn't it? Except that when she had said it, even to her the words had sounded flimsy and false. *The Nanny* is one of Pippa's favourite shows, but tonight the pleasure of mindlessly blobbing out in her usual Sunday-laid-back-luxury style while she waits for her dinner on a tray has been ruined.

Fran is wearing a tigerskin skirt and black high heels.
Maybe she should tell her mother the truth?

The butler is saying a really bitchy thing to the secretary.

Maybe Rosie and Asher were in some kind of danger?

Now there's a flashback to Fran's over-the-top mother sending her to camp in Israel.

What if Rosie and Asher got murdered like those hitch-hikers in New South Wales?

The butler scores some new cuff-links from the boss.

If they did it would all be her fault.

The secretary walks out in a huff.

But she had promised Rosie, promised and promised, to help lay a false trail.

Fran triumphs again, aided by butler and clever script writer.

Bloody hell, what on earth was she going to do?

Closing credits. Vera serves dinner with a crescendo of loud banging. Mince on toast and glaring looks. Bang. Smash. Crunch. Clunk. Whup. Thwack. Plop. How long can Pip hold out?

SUNDAY NIGHT ANXIETY MEDICINE

Malvina has tried:

1. Smoking four Winfield Ultra Lights in a row
2. Phoning Roger. Not home
3. Sara Lee Chocolate Obsession ice-cream. Quarter of a tub eaten with a teaspoon, standing at the sink
4. Hot bath with lavender and rose oils
5. Cheese sandwich with tomato lettuce and pickles
6. Writing furiously in her journal

7. Looking out the window and counting stars
8. Deep breathing
9. Yoga relaxation pose
10. The affirmation 'All is safe. I am at peace.'
11. Brandy. One tumbler full

HOW MALVINA FEELS

Drunk. Nauseous. Tired. Terrified.

MOON MEDICINE

Lily has tried:

1. A Valium
2. Crying noisily
3. A back rub from Robert
4. Switching TV channels over and over
5. Not eating her cream of chicken soup and toast
6. Phoning her sister, Melissa. It didn't help
7. A glass of chardonnay
8. Tidying Rosie's bedroom
9. Hugging Harry tightly
10. Crying softly
11. A sleeping pill

HOW SHE FEELS

Hungry. Drowsy. Numb. Terrified.

CAMPING AT CASTLE ROCK/ SUNDAY NIGHT

Asher gathers wood, dry blond pieces of sea debris. Leo makes a fire. Angel dresses up as Murglemurtle using a green velvet skirt for a cape and runs around yelling 'I'm scary, I'm scary' at the top of her voice. Star makes a big spicy soup. Rosie slices cheese and brown bread. The sunset is a red fiesta. The city has fallen away and nobody cares. The only question that gets asked is 'Who'd like some fruitcake?' and the answer is 'yes please' five times over.

LATER/TUCKED IN THEIR SLEEPING BAGS

Rosie and Asher have set up the silver dome near the kombi, looking out towards the gigantic red cliffs. It is wild and windy and they can hear waves thundering against rock. Sunset had opened with a burst of loud red, moved through a display of extravagant orange and dwindled to a ragged symphony of pink-and-gold wisps against deepest blue. Now the heavy blackness of night has swallowed all the colours up. There's something comforting about the faint glow from the van and the muffled sounds of radio and voices, and it is cosy tucked up in sleeping bags, alone again after the meal and the talking and the quiet, dreamy time by the fire.

PRELUDE

Rosie?

Mmm.

Do you like them?

Star and Leo and Angel? Yeah, I like them a lot.

It's good that they haven't asked us where we are going or anything.

They will though, don't you reckon?

Yeah, I do. They must be wondering about us.

Do you think we should tell them the truth?

I don't know. I mean, what else can we tell them?

We could say we're seventeen and we're youth hostelling around Australia, that our parents know where we are.

I doubt if they'd believe us.

What if we tell them the truth and they dob us in?

I don't think they would somehow.

Me neither. They seem pretty cool.

Shall we give it to them straight then . . . if they ask?

Yeah, I reckon.

Asher?

What?

All day I've been wondering . . .

Wondering what?

About kissing.

Kissing?

Yeah, if we're going to.

Oh. And?

I've decided.

Decided?

That we should. If you want to.

Oh.

So do you?

Want to kiss you?

Yeah.

Yes.

THE

The squirming of sleeping bags. The raging of hormones. The pounding of hearts. The meeting of lips. The touching of tongues. The crashing of waves. The gentle sleep of two tired travellers.

PIPPA'S DREAM

It smells like chocolate cake and patchouli oil and it's not in colour, but it's not in black and white, either. It is a sepia dream, golden brown like a faded photograph, and it begins gently. She and Rosie are swimming, not in the sea but in a river, a swift flowing river with smooth boulders and clear water, like the rivers she played in as a kid in New Zealand. They are wearing funny old-fashioned polka-dot bathing suits with ruffles and skirts, like fifties girls, and they are playing, splashing each other and laughing, their laughter as light as froth, floating up to meet the sky. Asher will be here soon on his motorbike, says Rosie, which somehow makes a watery kind of sense. And then the nibbling begins, a shoal of little fish nipping and biting around their ankles, and then more fish come and more fish. Too many fish, with rows of tiny bothery teeth, and the river bank seems far away, too far away to reach. Pippa wakes, tangled up in her green satin doona.

MONDAY MORNING AT THE COP SHOP

In a little grey room at Perth Police Headquarters, Constable Geoffrey Bannister is typing the Missing Persons information onto the police database. He is a very new constable and is not known as an intellectual giant, which is why he gets given huge piles of paperwork to do. No wonder he finds his job incredibly boring. Asher Bodhi Fielder, he types, no, darn it, that should be Fielding. Fifteen years old. Long dark hair, in dread-lock style. Height, weight, identifying marks, none, blah blah blah. Rosemary, damn, Rosie Elizabeth Moons, make that Moon, fifteen years old, long dark hair, height, weight, identifying marks, nose-ring — these two sound like the Bobsey twins. Leave space for photoscan, F2, press enter. To be sent to all stations between here and Adelaide, and to all stations on the eastern seaboard. Special Attention Sydney and Byron Bay. Press F8, save document and escape. Thank goodness it's time for a cuppa and a bikkie and a ciggie. This law and order is very demanding stuff.

MONDAY MORNING AT THE MOONS' HOUSE

Robert has gone to work. It doesn't feel right to go but what good will staying home do, he and Lily reason. Life must go on. Lily has driven Harry to school with a smile sellotaped to her lips, and now she is sitting at the kitchen table fiddling with the rose petals that have fallen onto the polished surface of the table. If she comes back, she thinks, no, *when* she comes back . . . when she comes back it will be different. I will hug her more and lecture her less. I will love her and cherish her and buy her a ruby for her nose. I will lie down in the mud and sing the Hallelujah Chorus if that's what it takes for us both to be happy. I will not sweat the small stuff and I'll try to remember that most of it is small stuff. If she comes back. When she comes back. If she comes back.

MONDAY MORNING/BLUFF KNOLL/ KALBARRI

There's nothing like a big bowl of porridge for breakfast. A big bowl of porridge with raisins cooked in it so they swell up plump and juicy. A big bowl of raisin-dotted porridge with runny honey drizzled on top and a sprinkling of slivered toasted almonds on top of that to give a delicious nutty crunch to each bite. A big bowl of hot, nutty, raisin porridge with a drizzle of honey and a big slosh of creamy organic soya milk, to be eaten by a smouldering campfire with the warmth of the sun on your back. A bowl of porridge and a cup of smoky tea and a companionable silence and a whole unknown day stretching tantalisingly ahead. Twenty miles out of town. A million miles from the life you left behind.

SPILLING THE BEANS

So, where are you kids actually headed?
Nowhere, really.
Nowhere?
Well, north. We're not sure. Broome, maybe. We've only got a week or so and then we have to go back.

Back to Perth?

Yeah.

Do your parents know where you are?

Not really.

Stranger and stranger. Are you going to give us the full story or what?

If you like. It's kind of complicated.

Well, in that case I think I'd better make us all another cup of tea.

MONDAY MORNING/STAFF ROOM/ BIRCH STREET HIGH

After seeing Mr McKenna and telling him that the wallet has been found, Mrs Hyde goes into the staff room. The last person she wants to see is Tim Epanomitis but there he is, slurping on his coffee and hogging the paper as usual. God, he annoys her. Always chewing on something, something fattening, and him as thin as a rake. What is it this morning? It looks like a fudge brownie, rich and moist and chocolatey, the creep. If there was any way she could avoid him knowing of her mistake about Asher and the wallet she would gladly take it, but as Mr McKenna will be making an announcement to the staff at morning-tea time, she feels it might alleviate her guilt if she bites the bullet and tells Asher's defender the story herself.

Hi, Tim, she says.

Hello, Wendy. Have a good weekend?

Fine, thanks. Actually something pretty major happened.

Oh?

My husband was cleaning my car and he found my wallet. It was stuck underneath the front seat. It must have slipped out of my bag on Friday morning. I can't have brought it in to school at all, although I was sure I had.

You *found* the wallet?

Yes, I feel pretty bad about it as a matter of fact. Mr McKenna and I are going to see Asher first period, apologise, admit our mistake.

That might be difficult.

Why?

I just got a phone call from Malvina Fielding, Asher's mother. He and Rosie Moon have run away, across the Nullarbor, heading to the eastern states. Haven't been seen since Friday night. It's pretty serious, police involvement, the full bit. He's had a pretty rough time settling in here, family break-up, new school, the works. The accusation was the last straw apparently.

Oh, my God.

Sit down, Wendy. Freaking out won't do anyone any good. Here, have a brownie.

ROCK DANCING/MONDAY SOMETIME

God, Leo, this place is amazing.

Isn't it stunning? The colours in these rocks are so beautiful.

Mmmm. So, they *are* runaways. I thought so.

Yeah, nice kids though. Look at them over there, horsing around with Angel — three crazy colts.

It would be a shame to send them back.

Risky not to, though.

Maybe not. From what they said no one will be looking for them up here.

True.

So if we took them with us for a bit, until it was time for them to split, no one would be any the wiser.

It's not very rational but I tend to agree. What harm would it do? Give them a bit of sanctuary. Life's tough when you're that age. It feels sort of cosmic to help them out.

Shall we?

Yeah, let them be gypsies for a little bit longer. Why the hell not?

TALKING WITH ANGEL

So are you going to come with us?

Yes, we are. For a week.

How many sleeps is a week?

Seven sleeps. This many fingers.

That's good. I like you guys and Murglemurtle does too. Are we going to Broomstick?

It's Broome, not Broomstick, but no, we're not going there. We thought we were but it's way too far. Leo showed us on a map, and Broome would take lots and lots of sleeps to get to. You guys are going to go up there later. We're all going to stay here for a few nights and then we're going to go to Monkey Mia to see the dolphins.

Are there monkeys there too?

No, only dolphins. And people, and fish, I guess.

Why is it called Monkey Minor then?

Monkey Mia. Well, I don't know. Do you, Ash?

Nah. But maybe we can find out when we get there.

Do you want to see my treasures?

Yes, we'd like that, wouldn't we?

Sure. Where are your treasures?

In my special tin.

So where's this special tin?

It's in my big pocket, silly.

Come on then, give us a look.

A TIN OF TREASURES:

3 glittery angel pictures

1 big whirly blue marble

2 crackled smarties, one purple, one yellow

A $100 bill in Monopoly money

A silvery green-and-blue parrot feather

A scrap of black satin with a poppy embroidered on it

A dried lizard

A headless Mighty Morph Power Ranger (Aisha)

PIPPA AT LUNCHTIME

Hi, Pip.

Hi, Emma.

Where's Rosie?

She's . . . she's not here today.

I can see that for myself, pea-brain. So where is she? She sick or something?

No, she's not sick. She's . . . gone away.

With her olds?

No.

Who with then?

Actually she's gone away with Asher.

You're kidding, right?

Nah.

Gone away . . . like *run* away?

Yeah, I guess.

So where are they?

God, Emma, how should I know? Get off my back, okay?

There's no need to get shitty. I mean, you're her best friend and everything. I was only asking.

Yeah, I know. It's just . . . it's a bit complicated, that's all.

Complicated?

Look. I don't want to talk about it, okay? It's freaking me out a bit, to be honest.

So, like, are they in Sydney or something?

Emma!

Yeah, I know, but wow, taken off with Asher, I mean, that's amazing. I didn't even know they were an item.

I hate that term. An item. They're just friends, that's all.

Oh, yeah, sure. Just friends and the sky is purple and pigs can fly. I hope they took some condoms.

Emma, for goodness sake!

What's the matter with that? Safe sex and everything. Or maybe she's on the pill. Susanne Drover is. Her mother got it for her.

Well, that's a relief.

God, this is amazing. Do the teachers know?

I guess so. I'm not sure.

I can't wait to tell everyone. It's not like, a secret, or anything?

Well, not really. You don't have to make a big thing of telling everyone, though. And don't say they're an item, okay?

And they've gone to Sydney, right?

I think . . . I think they might have.

This is wild. I mean, wow. Are you going to finish that roll, or what?

What? Oh, no. I'm not that hungry.

Can I have it then? I left my lunch at home.

Yeah, sure.

You don't have a dollar you could lend me, do you?

Nah.

Damn. I could really go for a Coke.

AFTER HIS MORNING TEA

Constable Geoffrey Bannister dawdled over his tea, white with two, and his government-ration Granita biscuit. His cigarette, taken outside the smoke-free building, tasted foul. He really should give up, he knew that, but the nicotine still had him by the balls. The regulation ten-minute break had stretched to fifteen but then Sergeant Parry had started giving him the hairy eyeball and there was nothing for it but to get back to work. If only he could remember what it was he was supposed to be doing next.

Bannister?

Yes, Sergeant?

These photographs were in my tray. The two kids you did the Missing Persons for this morning. Scan the photographs into the document and send out the report, all stations between here and Adelaide and all up the coast to Byron Bay.

Okay, but . . .

What is it?

I was just thinking. What if they didn't go in that direction? I mean, what if they were still in Perth or down at Margaret River or something?

We don't pay you to think, Bannister. The girl's best friend said they had headed east, she'd be a pretty reliable source, I would imagine. However, since you seem so keen to get involved, what about a bit of an inquiry? Last time the boy took off he got the seven o'clock bus to Adelaide. You could check with the driver from that particular run, just in case, see if he remembers them, phone all the roadhouses, see if you can get on their trail. It's not top priority but we should get on to it and I've got a meeting at one o'clock that could take up most of the afternoon. All right?

Yes, sir.

Good. Get cracking then.

ROSIE DAYDREAMING

What day is it? It must be Monday. We've only been gone since Friday and it feels like for ever. This place is great, these bizarre red rocks are like landscapes from a primitive world long before cities were even dreamed of. I don't remember it being like this. Maybe we never came to this part. It's lovely lying here in the sun. I'm a lizard. A big lizard in a rainbow dress with dirty feet and an enigmatic smile. Soon I'll go help Ash and Angel make that cubby-house but right now I just want to laze about. I really like being out in the wilderness, although I've got to have a wash soon for sure. Star said I could use the solar shower thingy if I like. She and Leo are so neat, so easy-going, not like Mum. Shit, I wish I hadn't thought about her, suddenly my belly feels tight and knotted. I don't want to give this up . . . it's special here, me and Ash and Star and Leo and funny little Angel, but I do miss home a bit too. I wonder what they told Harry, wonder how Pip is doing . . . God, she'll be sitting in Ancient History right now. I bet she misses me. I miss her, too. I wish she was here. Still, I have heaps to tell her when I do get back. Like about last night. The kiss. The kiss. The yummy scrummy kiss.

BUILDING

Here, fruitloop, hold this steady and I'll tie these together and then we'll have a roof.

Okey dokey spokey.

There. One cubby-house.

It's not a cubby-house. It's a Murglemurtle house.

A Murglemurtle house?

Yeah, dumb bum.

Dumb bum yourself. So, how come I haven't seen this Murglemurtle person?

She's not a person. She's a wicked princess. And *you* can't see her.

Why not?

Only me can see her.

Oh . . . a wicked princess?

Yeah, sometimes she's wicked.

What does she do?

She eats all the lollies and she watches television all the time and she calls people broccoli-brains and fuckface.

Drastic. And what does she do when she's not being wicked?

She does dancing and she plays with me.

That sounds like fun. But how come I can't see her?

Well, I dunno. Maybe you will one day. If . . .

If what?

I dunno. If you be quiet.

USELESSLY SLEUTHING

Hello, is that Mr Frederick Saunders?

Yes.

This is Constable Geoffrey Bannister from the Missing Persons Department, Perth CID. Greyhound Pioneer gave me your phone number. I'm hoping you might be able to help me with an inquiry we are doing at the moment. Two missing teenagers.

Sure, fire away.

Were you the driver of the Adelaide-bound coach that left Perth at seven o'clock on Friday night?

Yep.

The pair that we're looking for are fifteen years old, a girl and a boy, both on the tall side, long dark hair. The boy has dreadlocks, the girl has a nose-ring. Does that ring a bell?

No, mate. They weren't on the bus. No way.

Can you be sure about that?

Yeah, I'd remember them. That time in particular. We had a breakdown at Northam. The passengers had to get off and they all milled around while we waited, drank some coffee in the Shell roadhouse there. Mostly older people, couple of families, a snowy-haired backpacker from Germany or Austria or somewhere. Definitely not a pair of dark-haired teenagers. Not on that bus.

I see. Look, thanks a lot for your help.

Yeah, no worries, mate.

MONDAY AFTER SCHOOL

What's up with you, girl? That lip gets any lower we'll both trip over it.

Nothing, Mum.

Don't nothing me, Pippa Heke. What's up? Did something bad happen at school?

No, not really. It's just . . .

Just what?

Rosie, that's all. I miss her.

Yeah, must be hard without her all right. Didn't you have anyone to hang around with?

I had lunch with Emma. But . . . but it wasn't the same.
It won't be for ever, you know. They'll be back, back to face the music. Lily rang up this afternoon. Apparently Rosie rang her folks yesterday. They were out but she left a message on the answer-phone.
What did she say?
Said they would be coming back in a couple of weeks. Had to have some 'time out', if you please. Said the boy didn't nick anything.
Well, he didn't. Get this. Mrs Hyde found her wallet in her car. They made an announcement in the staff room today and Mr Epanomitis told his class and Thomas told Amy and Amy told me. Mum, what'll happen to them?
What do you mean?
When they come back. Will anything happen to them?
I don't know. Bloody good growling is one thing that should happen. Rosie will probably be grounded for about a thousand years.
They won't get sent away or anything, will they?
I doubt it. Rosie won't, I don't think. The boy, well, he's run away twice — might be a different story. Welfare might think his mother can't control him. Single parent and all that.
But that's so ridiculous.
You know that and I know that but we don't make the rules, kid. You got any homework tonight?
No, not really. I have to take a hat to school tomorrow for drama. We're doing characterisation.

Which hat are you going to take?
Can I take your straw one with flowers?
Yeah. Don't you dare lose it, though.
I won't.
Pip?
What?
Anything else you want to tell me, girl?

WILL SHE WON'T SHE

Pippa Heke is hiding out in her bedroom, sprawled on her bed amongst her collection of amazing animals. There's a purple velvet zebra, a one-eyed tiger, a green-haired troll, Daisy Duck who is actually a hot-water-bottle cover, and three bears who are all named Rupert. In the middle there is one worried girl with a ruby in her nose, her blue hair slicked tight onto her head with slippery coconut gel. She is wearing a fluffy pink-and-blue crochet midriff top and pale blue bellbottoms and she has two major worries going on in her head on parallel tracks. One is whether she should get her navel pierced. The other is should she tell the truth about Rosie.

Geez, I nearly did it. If the phone hadn't rung just then I'd have blurted it out for sure.
I wonder if getting it done would hurt more than it did when I got my nose pierced?
Mum knows I know something and she's not going to let up. She's cunning, like a snake, that woman. Knows just when to strike.
Angela had hers done but it just kept coming out.

That dream. It made me feel really anxious.

I wonder if it would rub against my clothes and be annoying. In my jeans it could be a real drag.

My grandmother was known far and wide as a famous psychic. Maybe I am too. Maybe the universe is trying to warn me about something?

Anyway, I don't have fifteen bucks so maybe I'll leave it for a week or two.

Maybe I'm just fussing about nothing. They're probably having a really great time.

Hey, but I wonder what one would look like in my eyebrow?

I did promise I wouldn't tell. I promised.

Think I'll get something to eat and watch TV. I can't decide now because I'm hungry and it's too much of a hassle.

Think I'll get something to eat and watch TV. I can't decide now because I'm hungry and it's too much of a hassle.

BLISS

They played hide-and-seek, yelling wildly.

They had cheesy rice for lunch, with tomatoes and basil.

They fished on the rocks and caught a thong.

They made card-houses. Leo was the champion.

They walked on the rocks and got wet with wave spray.

They had crumpets and honey for afternoon tea.

They saw a rainbow, a faint one, out at sea.

Star did some embroidery, purple flowers on white calico.

Leo read *Zen Mind Beginner's Mind*.

Rosie and Angel drew wicked princess pictures.

Asher played twelve-bar blues on Leo's guitar.

ASHER

good guitar this better than mine i remember when we got mine it used to belong to mitchell me and dad did it up we sanded it down with the wet-dry paper it took for ever then we varnished it and it came up shiny and perfect i got the carry-case and the strap for my birthday birthday birthday oh shit no it can't be i think mum's birthday is coming up the twenty-fifth hell it can't be far off i'll have to talk to rosie damn and blast poor mum now that the buzz of leaving is over i have to admit i feel bad about taking off again it felt right at the time but now it doesn't feel so good mum will be worried and miserable specially on her birthday we always had a neat time on birthdays what about when dad tried to make a cake and it looked okay but it tasted dreadful because he tried to be creative and he put all those spices in it and lots of caraway seeds and poppy seeds but the birds liked it and then we went out and had chocolate cheesecake at the lotus cafe instead and mum was all happy because dad had tried so hard mum's birthday what am i going to do poop damn and blast leaving is one thing but going back now that is going to be something else

GEOFFREY BANNISTER TRIES HIS HARDEST

Eight roadhouses later and no wiser than he ever was. Three cigarettes, two cups of coffee and a meat pie down the track and he's still in the dark. A can of Pepsi and a call to the man at the Fruit Fly Inspection Depot at Eucla and still nothing. It didn't make sense. If these two airheads had headed out on Friday night someone would have seen them by now, surely? Maybe he wasn't Albert Einstein but this didn't make sense. At training school they were told that good detective work was a combination of common sense, hard work and intuition. Fancy Parry telling him he wasn't being paid to think. Here he is, using his common sense and intuition to the best of his ability, and all he gets is rubbished for it. Honestly, Parry could do with a refresher course in modern police applications.

Jeez, look at the time. Three forty-five. Geoffrey feels like plonking his snowstorm paperweight on top of all his papers, heading out the door and leaving the whole darned lot until tomorrow. Ah well, he knows another way of travelling to a place beyond the dreary beige walls of this room. Seven-and-a-half minutes later Geoffrey is happily staring into space, thinking wonderful thoughts about Rachel, the nice friendly receptionist at The Body Club, when the phone rings.

Bannister?

Yes, Sergeant?

Sorry I didn't make it back. Useless restructuring meeting. Lot of waffle and hot air. Any luck with the search?

No. None at all. Definitely not on the bus and not one sighting at any of the roadhouses.

Okay. I want you to get on to the *West Australian* and the television newsrooms. Little story on the front page tomorrow and small slots on the evening news at each of the stations tonight if you can get it. Should be time if you hurry. Give it a shot.

What about the photographs?

Scan them in again and send them on the Internet. Liz in publicity can show you how, if you need help. Let the journos know that this is not a suspected homicide, just two runaways. Better get on to it, though . . . it's a dangerous world out there. Bloody thoughtless kids.

JUST ON SUNSET/ROSIE HAS A SHOWER

I feel good. Alive and fresh and clean. I'm glad I got to use the solar shower. Asher settled for half a bucket of cold water but I like mine warmed by the sun. Short hair is so easy to wash. I'll wring out my dress and hang it on top of the tent to dry. Better get a peg from Star or it might blow away in the night. So windy here. Maybe we should have gone swimming with the others but I feel really lazy. Tomorrow we're off to Monkey Mia so having some mooching around time has been nice. What shall I put on? Good old jeans and black jumper and a squirt of perfume. Now I smell beautiful. Okay. All done. I'll go and help Asher gather wood.

MOMENT OF TRUTH

Feel better?

Sure do. It's great to be clean.

Yeah.

So, Monkey Mia tomorrow.

Yeah.

Are you okay, Asher?

Why do you ask?

You seem kind of sad or something.

To be honest, I've been wondering whether we should go back to Perth instead of going to Monkey Mia tomorrow with Star and Leo.

What? How come?

It feels all wrong, suddenly. I've been thinking it through. Maybe taking off isn't going to solve anything. My homesickness, the school, the accusation, it'll still be there when I get back. And now that the dust has settled I feel kind of yuck about my mother. Without my dad around she's going to be finding this really hard.

Oh.

I had this flash . . . I remembered that her birthday is coming up. Next week, I think. That's what got me thinking.

Wow, you want to head back tomorrow, not keep going?

Yeah, I guess. I mean, going back feels wrong but going on feels worse.

Yeah. I understand. It's just . . .

Just what?

I'm going to cop such a huge amount of hassle when I get back, you can't imagine. I probably won't be able to see you again or anything. My mother will come down really heavy about this.

Maybe if we go back earlier we'll cop less flak?

Maybe. Nah, you don't know my mother. She's . . . like, when she gets worried about anything she doesn't just worry, she gets hysterical. For example, when dad comes home late and she thinks that he's had an accident, she doesn't say, 'I'm glad you're home 'cause I've been really worried.' She says, 'Where the hell have you been?' She just loses it. She'll be totally vicious about this, I know for a fact. I won't be able to see you or anything.

They can't stop us. We'll see each other at school and when things settle down we'll get to see each other, for sure.

I didn't mean just at school.

I know. I want to see you, Rosie. At school. Out of school. Upside-down and totally. But I don't want to keep running.

Yeah, well, I guess. If you really think so. Do you think we should ring them or what? Or just turn up?

I reckon . . . look, here come Star and Leo. I wonder where Angel is?

TROUBLE

Hey, you guys.

Hi, Star. Leo. How was the beach?

Great. The water was . . . refreshing . . . to say the least.

Refreshing my arse, snorted Leo. It was freezing. So, where's Angel?

What do you mean? She went to the beach with you.

Yeah, but she came back. She started to grizzle and carry on about wanting to play with you two when we got half way down the track, so we let her come back.

But she didn't. She isn't here. Asher's been gathering wood . . . I went for a bit of a walk and then I had a shower . . . Angel isn't here.

Oh, God . . . no.

Don't panic, Star. Look, this is extraordinary. There's nowhere

she could have got lost between here and the beach.
Well, where is she then? What are we going to do, Leo? It's nearly dark.
Everyone spread out. Give it fifteen minutes and we'll meet back here, okay?
Sure.
Yeah.
Okay. I'll head back to the beach. Star, you check the van. Asher, over there and Rosie, that way, okay?

PANIC

Four people are running into the darkening dusk, their voices as crazy as shadows. Angel, they yell. Cooee. Cooee. Angel, Aaaangel. Where are you? No reply. Nothing. Only the fearful echo of their own noise, the wild pounding of the heart, the thunder of waves on rock. Nothing but the inky night creeping and curling around them, as itchy as a madman's cloak.

SEVEN O'CLOCK NEWS

Best time of the day this, thinks John Diamond. Well, the second best, anyhow. His favourite time of the day is the early morning when he sits on the verandah with the dogs at his feet, drinking a mug of strong tea, quietly watching the pale colours of dawn light up the sky; getting a feel for the weather. So quiet you can hear yourself change your mind. But this time of the day comes a pretty close second. The ease of it, the hard work of the day done, a good feed in his belly, putting his feet up and watching the seven o'clock news. Molly pottering around in the kitchen about to bring in a tray with a pot of tea and a couple of pieces of fruitcake on it. A chance to catch up on the world beyond dry red earth and tractors that break down and sheep that get through the fence. So what are the lily-livered politicians dilly dallying over tonight then, oh, that'd be right . . . you wouldn't think they had the nerve so soon after the elections, bloody crooks in suits, all of them. And now, the local news. Two teenagers have gone missing and are thought to be headed for Byron Bay, now where the hell was that exactly, somewhere just south of Sydney if he remembered rightly, or was that Jervis Bay? No, come to think of it that was Jervis Bay, darned good fishing down that way, too, if he recalled — hey, now wait a minute, blow me down, they looked a lot like those two he gave a lift to on Saturday. Hard to be a hundred per cent certain without his glasses on, and the hair was different, they must have shorn it off and done something to the colour, the little blighters — but he'd eat his favourite hat with a knife and fork if those weren't the very same ones. Told Molly when I got home that there was something iffy going on with those two, hitching off into the wide blue yonder and then suddenly changing their minds. That old I-feel-sick trick wouldn't fool a rabbit. Wouldn't say where they were headed. Couple of Geraldton kids fart-arsing around, that's what he'd thought then. Bloody hell, runaways from Perth, now how about that. Well, it could wait till after the sport and the weather and then he'd be making a phone call to the police, and that was for sure. Molly, he yells, what are you up to, my beauty, get yourself in here. You know those hitch-hikers . . .

KALBARRI POLICE STATION/ 7.00pm

Missing Person Report. Angel Parker-Stanford. Four years old. Lost between beach and camp site. Volunteer search party urgently required.

PERTH MISSING PERSONS BUREAU/ 7.35pm

Re: A. Fielding and R. Moon. File Number 74837.17496. Confirmed sighting just out of Geraldton, Saturday night. Mr John Diamond. (099) 564 711. Note: caller stated that the pair now have short blond hair.

PERTH MISSING PERSONS BUREAU/ 7.45pm

Re: A. Fielding and R. Moon. File Number 74837.17496. Confirmed sighting. Given lift in to Geraldton Sunday morning. Mrs Miriam Perkins. (099) 747 650. Note: Both individuals now have short bleached hair, confirming the above.

PERTH MISSING PERSONS BUREAU/ 7.50pm

Mrs Fielding and Mr and Mrs Moon informed.

PERTH MISSING PERSONS BUREAU/ 8pm

All police stations between Geraldton and Carnarvon informed.

HARRY IN BED/8.30pm

Mum's crying but Dad told me not to worry because it's happy crying that she's doing. The police rang up and said Rosie has been found, up north near Geraldton. I went there once but I can't remember it because I was only little. Well actually Dad said that Rosie hasn't quite been found but she *nearly* has. First they thought she went east but actually she went north. Dad showed me on the map. And get this, her hair is going to be different, short and bleached like a punk. Wow. Cool.

I'm glad she'll be home soon. It's been double-dipped yuckville here ever since she went away. Mum's been doing a lot of crying, the sad sort of crying, and Dad has tried to be cheerful only he isn't cheerful, and Mum keeps hugging me until I can't breathe properly. Even Beethoven has been skulking around looking drastic. Cats are pretty clever really. The good thing has been that Mum has let Beethoven sleep on my bed. Also, Simon Mears swapped me a Flake bar for a basketball card. It's quite squashed but I'm going to save it for Rosie. Even though it is crumbly it will still taste good. She can lick it off the wrapper, but knowing her she will eat it with a teaspoon or something.

THE MIRROR AND MALVINA

She puts on her black velvet leggings, her black t-shirt and her purple velvet coat embroidered with golden hearts. She puts on the perfume that makes her smell like a gardenia. She puts on her soft black leather boots and she heads out into the night.

MONDAY NIGHT/10pm/PERTH AIRPORT

A man with a grey ponytail carrying an old leather tote bag gets off a plane. His name is Nigel. A woman with golden moon earrings is there to meet him. Her name is Malvina.

HOT CHOCOLATE AT GINO'S/ FREMANTLE/10.40pm

Short blond hair! The ratbags. Oh, well, at least we know they're safe and roughly where they are.

The police were confident they'd find them in the next day or so. They can't have got much further than Geraldton. Kalbarri, the man said. Probably Kalbarri, but no further north than Carnarvon.

So, what happens then, once they're found?

Well, the police will hand them over to the Department of Community Services and they'll put them on a bus back to Perth. Then a social worker will come around and see us, sort a few things out, get Asher some counselling. The policeman who rang was really nice actually.

Right. So all we can do is wait it out then. Look, I'm knackered. I've got to get some sleep. How about you?

Yeah, I'm pretty pooped.

Come on, Mal. Let's go home.

MIDNIGHT/KALBARRI POLICE POST

His cup of coffee is getting cold but it's wet and sweet and it tastes just fine. Constable Dave Walker hopes he doesn't have a night like this one again for quite some time. Ever again actually. Thank goodness the missing kid turned up. It hadn't been looking good there for a while. The whole scenario had a very nasty feel about it in the beginning. Volunteers racing around every which way in the dark, worse than useless some of them, although Robbo was a good bloke. No sign of the missing kid. Absolutely no place she could have got to in that low-lying scrub. Waves crashing on rocks in the darkness, the sinking feeling in the guts as the minutes went by. Drowning was the obvious conclusion. Kid must have fallen off the rocks and been washed out to sea. They were all thinking it. The mother hysterical. The father silent. And then, as if that wasn't enough, the news coming in on his mobile that the two teenagers were runaways from Perth. He'd thought they were the couple's older children. No one had told him any different. 'Go and pack your gear, chums,' he'd said to them after the phone call, trying to stay steady in the midst of the chaos. The white face of the girl, the boy blurting out, 'But we want to help find Angel.' 'Sorry, mate. Go and pack up the tent. I'll drive you back to the police station,' he'd said, sounding more sensible than he felt, and off they'd shuffled.

And a good thing he *had* made that decision because, blow me down with a feather, there in the tent was the lost kid. She'd wandered back to the camp and by a twist of fate she hadn't seen the teenagers and they hadn't seen her, so she'd gone into their tent to have a bit of a poke around. She'd dressed up in their clothes, fossicked around, drawn a few pictures, and then she must have dozed off. Woke up when the boy stuck his head into the tent. There she was, sitting up all cool, calm and collected. Quite the little madam. I'm all right, she'd said. Nothing bad can happen to me. Murgley is looking after me, or something to that effect. Invisible friend apparently. Odd bods, these hippies with their strange names and ragged clothing. Maybe they didn't call them hippies any more. Probably call them ferals these days. Funny old world we live in. Still, it takes all sorts. The main thing was that the kid had been found.

But the fun wasn't over yet. Not with two runaway fifteen-year-olds asleep in the cells. He'd drive them back to Geraldton tomorrow. Hand them over to the Department of Community Services people who'd put them on the next bus back to Perth, unless the parents showed up. He'd better wash up the cups and fill out the log book, then do the rest of the paperwork. He could see that he wasn't going to get much sleep tonight.

ROSIE / WAKING

Here I am in a small ghastly room painted dreary government grey. Just a single bed with a scratchy grey blanket, a window looking out on to a deserted laneway, a toilet and a handbasin. Nothing else, that's it. It must be early in the morning but I've been awake for ages. I kept waking up because the foam mattress is thin and it was really uncomfortable. Also my feet were cold. My feet are *still* cold.

I feel dreadful; lonely and sad and empty. Today the cop is going to drive us to Geraldton and then some social worker is going to send us home on a bus. Mum is going to absolutely kill me, I know it, and I'll never get to see Asher again. They'll probably send me to boarding school or something.

During the night I had a bad dream. Mum and Dad and Harry and Pip were going somewhere important. They were all dressed up in their best clothes. Dad had a suit on and Mum was wearing a hat. Mum never wears hats. Harry's hair was all slicked down and his shoes were as shiny as glass. Pip had a black-and-white outfit on; she looked like a penguin. I was there too but I was invisible. Everyone just carried on talking and then they got into a limousine and drove off without me. No wonder I feel dreadful. I miss Asher already. I'll never see Star and Leo and Angel again. I'm tired and I'm hungry and I feel like I don't belong anywhere. This is the pits.

ASHER / WAKING

what's that noise where the heck am i oh no that's right the police station man i never thought it would turn out like this at least we found angel what an amazing kid she didn't have a clue what all the fuss was about there she was sitting up all fresh and perky in my stripey jacket with rosie's scarf wrapped around her head all smiles star and leo were beside themselves we all were it was hard saying goodbye to them leo got my address said he'd send me a postcard gave me a big bear hug he's a cool guy leo this room is dismal wonder where they got such a depressing shade of paint is there a world beyond grey i'm in a cell man i wonder what we'll get for breakfast i reckon i can smell bacon frying wouldn't care if it was fried shoe i'd probably eat it didn't get any dinner last night just a cup of tea and a tim tam then they took my belt as if i'd hang myself bizarre i wonder how rosie is last night she cried on the way here in the car i nearly did too overwhelmed the whole shebang just toppled down on us now we have to go back and face the music wonder what day it is i think it might be tuesday

HARRY

Today is a very good day. Rosie and that guy have been found. Mum and Dad got a call early this morning from a policeman. I was still asleep. When I woke up Mum told me and she is over-the-moon happy. Usually when she wakes me she is dressed because she's been jogging and Dad has already left for work, but this morning they were both still in their dressing gowns and we all had breakfast together. Mum poured me two lots of orange juice. Also I was dipping my raisin toast into Dad's cup of tea and she didn't even notice. Tonight after dinner we are going to go and meet the bus. I can't wait to see Rosie and her hair. Last night in bed I got a bit peckish and ate some of the Flake bar but there's a bit left. I don't suppose Rosie will mind. I bet she throws a wobbly when she finds out that Beethoven sleeps with me now. She will say that it is totally unfair because Mum never lets her have the cat in her room. But I will let her have a turn when I sleep over at Ted's house.

BREAKFAST AT GINO'S

Malvina

Nigel

One sleepy waiter

One flat white

One cappuccino

Two glasses of water

One bagel with scrambled eggs

One muesli, fruit salad and yoghurt

One crumpled *West Australian* newspaper

Smiles

Tenderness. Joy. Delight.

A little spilt coffee on a bill for $16.95

HEADING SOUTH/9am

Constable Dave Walker feels like a prat. He is sitting by himself in the front seat of the car and the two kids are in the back seat. He feels embarrassed, a spare part, a fifth wheel. His plan had been to make the boy sit in the front and the girl sit in the back but before he'd had time to say anything, bingo, they had both hopped into the back. Ah well, he didn't blame them. There was no way he'd want to be separated if he was them. It would probably be the last chance they got to be together for quite some time after this day was over. The parents were going to shorten the rope for these two, if they had any sense. Limits and boundaries, that's what teenagers needed. If he ever had kids . . . pretty unlikely, seeing he didn't even have a girlfriend

. . . these two rascals were rather sweet, though. Look at them, snuggled up together, the boy with his arm around the girl, her head leaning on his shoulder. They look tired and sad.

Tired. Like him. He had managed to get a few hours sleep but he still felt ragged. The morning coffee and fried eggs sat uneasily in his guts. It was going to be a long day. A hundred and sixty-seven kilometres to Geraldton, some mucking about at the Department of Community Services, and a hundred and sixty-seven kilometres back again. Better put the radio on to keep himself company.

CASTLES IN THE AIR

Ash?

Mmm.

I thought of a good one.

Good one?

Band name. Love Struck Chord.

Yeah, great.

How about The Incredibles?

Yeah. Road Monsters.

Sunflowers.

Purple Delusion.

Double-dipped Nerds.

The Planet Waves.

Fat Girl Pirates.

Potato.

Nah, not potato. You can't call a band that.

Rosie?

Mmmm.

It'll work out.

Yeah, maybe. Ash?

What?

I'm still glad we did it.

Really?

Yeah. It's been great. Our awfully big adventure. I mean, I'm kind of glad to be going home but I'll miss you.

We'll still see each other.

I hope so. But I'll miss you at night. I'll have to go back to sleeping with Hartley.

Hartley?

My beloved Hartley. It won't be the same. He's my panda.

Rosie, you're mad.

Good mad?

The best.

You are too. Better than Hartley. Better than anyone. The very best.

TRAVELLING ON

Sometime in the late morning they set off, Star and Leo and Angel and Murglemurtle, in the blue VW kombi, heading north. For breakfast they toasted the last of the bread on the campfire. When everything was packed they began. First, they made a circle of rocks. Next they gathered tiny yellow wildflowers and seed pods and made an inner circle, and inside that they fashioned a heart using dusty red pebbles. This is a special place, said Leo. A place of gratitude. A place where loss and hope danced a jig and the right guy won. We give thanks for the gift of Angel's safety. Star played 'Amazing Grace' on her flute. Angel got her whirly blue marble out of the tin and placed it carefully in the very middle of the red heart. And then they got into the van and drove onwards.

AT THE BOOKSHOP

Hi. Sorry I'm so late.

Morning, Mal. What's up?

Do you want the good news first or the best news?

I want the lot. Sock it to me, baby.

It's Asher. He and Rosie have been found. They were up at Kalbarri, camping out with a hippie couple who had a little girl. The girl went missing but it's okay, they found her. I don't know all the details, but the main thing is that Asher and Rosie will be back tonight. Nine o'clock at the bus depot.

Wonderful. How terrific that he's safe.

But that's not all. Get this! Nigel's here. He flew in last night. It's so good to see him. You can't imagine how good.

I probably can, you know. No wonder you're all flushed and radiant. Nothing like a bit of good old-fashioned bonking to lift the spirits, is there, sweet pea?

Roger, you are quite dreadful.

I do my best. Now, are you going to sort out an invoice for that ghastly big order or am I?

LILY ON THE BEACH

Deserted. No one else there this morning, not even the fat guy, the wobbly star-jump man. Just her and the blue sky. Lily feels terrific. Rosie is coming home. Funny how things turn out. Clouds and silver linings. If everything hadn't got so awful between them she'd never have started seeing Dr Parker, which has been such a challenging but positive thing. And Rosie running away, even though it has been traumatic, has somehow brought her and Robert closer again. Sharing feelings, late-night cuddles, managing to survive it together . . . it felt like they were friends again. For the first time in ages Lily feels totally alive and happy. The sun is shining. Rosie is coming home.

SUDDENLY

What? Swerving. Impact. No. Inside a washing machine. Whirling. Catapulting. Red. Orange. Stars. Smoke. Burning rubber. Stench. Please no. Beyond anywhere. Leg. Chest. Wet. Numb. Help me. Screaming. Whimpering. Black. Nothing. Nowhere.

SOMETIMES

Sometimes you think you know where you are headed. You think you know what each day will bring. You think there will be a breath to follow this breath. It has always been that way before. You think that lunch will follow breakfast and sometime later dinner will naturally appear. You think you know that the sky is blue and that trees are green, that cats are furry and that life will go on quite smoothly for ever like an infinite ripple of turquoise ribbon. But sometimes you are wrong.

GERALDTON HOSPITAL/NOON

In the Accident and Emergency Room, Dr Prakash is taking a well-earned breather. What a hectic morning. One skateboarder with a double fracture, one sliver of metal to be removed from an eye, a diabetic coma needing medication, and a badly gashed finger to suture. The phone rings. Damn. It is going to be a very short breather. Bad accident. Three bodies. Ten minutes.

ASHER

no no please no accident nightmare my chest hurts blood all over me thick sticky blood rosie no rosie help she won't wake up her head is bleeding everywhere the man i think he's dead he can't be dead he was a nice man we were just driving along not far to go kids he said i was nearly asleep long drive the radio playing crap music what's happened mum help blood rosie rosie no please no

☎ EMERGENCY

Royal Flying Doctor Operations Room. Can I help you?
This is Dr Chandra Prakash speaking. Accident and Emergency Department at Geraldton Hospital. We've had a major road accident here, three people injured. This is a request to get two of the patients to Royal Perth immediately. One is a head-injury case. I'm not sure of the extent of the injury but I see this as a Priority One. A pressurized aircraft is required and it'll need to be doctor-accompanied. The other patient is a fractured rib,

possible lung puncture, shock. He's a Priority Three but I'd like to get him to Royal Perth for further assessment.

Right you are. I'll need to call Meekatharra Base on this one. I don't think they had a job on this morning but I'll just ring through and check. Hold the line, please — Dr Prakash?

Yes?

All systems go. The plane and doctor from the base at Meekatharra are on their way. They should be in Geraldton in forty-five minutes. Can you get the patients by ambulance to the hangar at one forty-five?

We'll be there.

Right you are, then. We'll have an ambulance standing by at Jandakot to get them to Royal Perth.

Great. Thank you.

Cheers. Goodbye now.

HARRY

Something's wrong. Mum didn't pick me up from school. Ned's mother did. She gave us a snack of corn chips and orange juice and we're allowed to go on the computer but I don't want to. Ned said I can ride his bike if I like but I don't feel like it. We played with his rabbit and the fur made me sneeze. Stupid rabbit. It scratches. I don't want to play. I want to go home. Ned's mother says that Rosie has been in an accident and that everything will be fine. But her lips go thin when she says it and she won't look at me properly. It must be bad. I don't know where Rosie is and I don't know where Mum is. Ned is an idiot.

He keeps on tickling the rabbit and it doesn't like it. His mother says I am staying the night. She keeps calling me dear. I want to go home.

INFINITY

Golden light. Tunnelling. Not stopping. Just like Alice. Through the looking glass. Drifting and floating and flying. I am a white dove flying. I am flying sleek-winged above a garden, above a maze, above flower beds. Hollyhocks and roses. A garden rake. Flying. Lost. Cold. Ice. I am the Ice Princess. I am a skeleton. I am white bones. I am drifting and drifting. Crystals. Silent in the crisp snow. Let go. Easier to let go. I am going. The panda bear says no with his sad eyes. He is calling my name.

ASHER/WARD TWO/7pm

pethidine is what the nurse gave me shirley she is fat she is kind i feel strange i am sleepy and warm dad is here how did dad get here i am not dreaming i don't think he and mum went to get something to eat i told them about the plane it was a conquest white with a blue stripe it was very small inside it was like being in a van two seats and two stretchers the doctor and the flying nurse sat on the seats i was on one stretcher rosie was on the other one she didn't wake up rosie wake up her hair all stuck together brown with dried blood like mud dad said not to worry son they are looking after rosie please let her be all right first the plane was noisy then it was quiet there were oxygen masks and bottles we lost all our stuff maybe someone will send it my silver dome is gone the policeman his name was dave don't let him be dead dad is here how did dad get here warm as toast my feet feel lazy everything is very strange

LATE AT NIGHT

In the weird bright light of the hospital corridor Lily and Robert meet Malvina and Nigel. Lily is clutching a polystyrene cup of murky liquid which bears no resemblance whatsoever to coffee. No one knows quite what to do, or say. Robert shakes Nigel's hand. Lily and Malvina try to smile at each other, fighting off the tiredness and the tears. Clumsy words are passed back and forth. Broken rib. Lucky. He's asleep now. She's still unconscious. Tests. Know more in the morning. In our prayers. Take care then. Goodnight.

LILY

Dear God, let Rosie survive. I'll do anything. Whatever it takes. Look after my Rosie. She's got her whole life ahead of her. She's a good kid. This world needs people like her. When she was little she tried to wrap up her dinner in a towel to send to the poor people. She was full of laughter and light. Dancing and playing all day long. Writing stories and reading them to us so seriously. The Magic Umbrella, by Rosie Elizabeth Moon. Taking Harry for walks in his pram. One time she brought him back with red hibiscus flowers arranged all over his blanket and one tucked behind his ear. He didn't even wake up. That kid. Dressing up Beethoven in my best underwear. I don't care about the nose-ring. I don't care about the fighting. I don't care about anything, God. I don't care what you ask of me, but you have to give Rosie back. Just do it. I'm not asking. I'm telling.

MIDNIGHT/CHANGE OF SHIFT

Hi, Shirley. What sort of a night has it been?

Not too bad actually. It was busy earlier but it's gone quiet now.

What do I need to know?

It's all on the charts. The woman in bed seven is in a lot of pain, morphine two hourly. Teenage girl in bed eleven, flown in from up north with a suspected fractured skull. With a bit of luck it'll be only a scalp bleed and concussion — still waiting on full test results but Doctor Page said it's looking hopeful. Her vital signs are stable. She might wake up soon, she'll be pretty out of it though. Her parents are with her.

Righty-oh.

I'm out of here. I've got a date with a hot bath and a pair of red-and-white pyjamas.

See ya, Shirl.

MORNING/ASHER

early six-thirty the ward is alive with rattles and bangs nurse woke me up took my temperature shirley is off duty this one is steven he's got three gold earrings in one ear quite a cool guy he said mum and dad went home to get some sleep they'll be back after breakfast i've got a fractured rib it aches bandaged not plaster i'm allowed to go to the toilet by myself and walk around if i take it gently the man in the bed next to me has a tube up his nose he's making a rather revolting wheezing noise i hope mum brings me a t-shirt and my track pants to wear this silly white gown doesn't have a proper back on it i hope she doesn't buy me pyjamas only little kids and old men wear pyjamas steven doesn't know how rosie is but he said he'd find out for me i told him it is very urgent last night i was terrified but now it is day and everything feels brighter she just has to be okay here comes a pink-uniformed lady with massive boobs the hot-drink trolley milo please i feel woozy must be the peth they gave me quite an odd feeling sort of spacy but underneath that i am battered and bruised my chest is bandaged up too tightly aching and what i want to know is what about rosie?

BIZARRE

A market or a bazaar. Colourful. People everywhere. Twittering bird song. Yellow budgies and rainbow finches swooping and diving. A flower stall with violets and pansies and freesias done up in bright bouquets with pink and purple tissue paper. A land of a thousand dances. An elegant fountain with pale blue and pink cascades of water. A sculpture made of huge coloured pencils. Little boys selling chestnuts and oranges. A gypsy man in striped satin pantaloons singing opera. Three white poodles. A table of hats, old ones made of felt and roses and ribbons. Rows of paper dolls. Delicate shoes with curly toes and tiny bells on. Turrets. Windows. Doorways. Sunlight fading into dusk. Shadows. I don't know where I am. A strange hard bed. Lying down. Headache. Someone is holding my hand and stroking it.

LILY AND ROSIE

Mum, Mum . . .

It's all right, darling. I'm here. Dad's here too.

What happened?

A car accident. You were on your way home and the policeman fell asleep at the wheel. You're in Royal Perth Hospital. It's all right now. You're safe. Everything's all right.

What about Asher?

He's okay. He has a fractured rib but he's fine.

Where is he?

He's in ward seven. He's fine. Asher's fine.

Can I see him?

Later, sweetheart.

What about the policeman?

He's okay, darling. Some broken bones. Don't you worry. It's going to be fine. There, there, you have a good cry. Robert, will you go and get the nurse, please? They'll probably want to check her now she's awake.

WHAT MALVINA AND NIGEL BRING ASHER

a bar of Energy chocolate

a *Mad* comic

three mandarins

Nigel's tartan night-shirt

WHAT ASHER SAYS

I'm not wearing that thing.

Why not, hon?

Nah. It might look good on an old fart like you, Dad, but there's no way I'm wearing it. I'd look like a peanut.

Don't you want the nurses to see those gorgeous long legs of yours?

Don't tease him, Nigel. Would you wear a pair of pyjamas, then?

Nah, no way. Anyway, the nurse said I can go home today, after the doctor has made his rounds.

When will that be?

About two o'clock.

Great. Fantastic. So, how are you feeling?

Okay. A bit sore. Mum, how's Rosie? The nurse said he'd find out for me but he's been really busy.

I don't know, love. We came straight here. Last night she was in a stable condition. We met her mum and dad in the corridor.

Can you go and find out?

What do you think, Nigel?

Yeah, why not. Do you want me to come with you?

No, I'll go. You stay here with Ash.

PIPPA

Rosie's been in a car accident. She's in hospital but she's going to be okay. Her mum rang this morning. I'm allowed to leave school at lunchtime and go and visit her. I'm taking my pink bellbottoms and my silver stretchy top. I can't wait to see her. Thank goodness she's okay. I can't wait to see her hair. Can't wait to show her my new colour. Can't wait to hear about everything. What an adventure. I wonder if she boofed him?

ROSIE/LUNCHTIME

So that was a hospital lunch: soup and mashed potato. Usually you put in a form and tick the boxes but I'm on light food for the first twenty-four hours. Before lunch I had a shower. The nurse helped me because I'm still very wobbly. My hair was a mess, all matted with dried blood. They had to shave a bit off around the cut but it doesn't look too bad. I've still got a massive headache and one of my legs is a mess, all red and swollen. I have to stay here for observation and some tests, and the day after tomorrow I can go home. Dad and Mum have left but Mum is going to bring Harry in to visit me this afternoon and Dad will come after work. I want to see Asher but the nurse said I have to stay put. I wonder why he hasn't come to see me.

ASHER

not going up in this stupid white gown not wearing the tartan thing dad was right my legs are so skinny i would look like an idiot mum took my clothes she's going to bring some clean ones to go home in she and dad will be back later to pick me up what can i wear then do i dare well what else can i do he won't mind he's in la-la land he doesn't need them excuse me grandpop it's only a borrow just what i always wanted a brown striped woollen dressing gown never mind steven is up at the other end of the ward with the man who keeps calling out so i'll just casually head for the toilet see you grandpop nice and easy off i go out the swing doors past the lifts and up the stairs nice and gently that's the ticket yikes this floor is very cold

GREETINGS EARTHLING

Hey.

Hey yourself.

I wondered if you'd come.

I wanted to come earlier but I had to find something to wear that didn't show my bum to the world. I scored this from the old bloke in the bed next to me. Like it?

Groovy. My mum's going to bring my nightie later. The white hospital gown isn't much of a fashion look, is it?

No way. I brought you this. Are you okay?

Pretty much. I've got a headache and I feel weak but the nurse said that's normal. I have to stay here a couple of days for observation and tests. How about you?

I'm fine. My chest is bandaged up, that's all. I'm being discharged later. That's why I sneaked up now. I have to go back soon for the doctor's round.

I'm so glad to see you, Ash. God, it's all so weird.

Yeah. I thought you were dead. On the plane you just lay there. There was blood everywhere.

I don't remember anything. Only the car swerving. Then nothing. Just these amazing strange dreams.

We're lucky to be alive.

Yeah, so is the policeman, my dad told me. Very lucky. He's in Geraldton Hospital with multiple fractures.

Maybe we can send him a card.

Sure. It doesn't seem real, does it, Ash?

No . . . Oh drat, that nurse is giving me the hairy eyeball. I've got to scoot before I get chucked out of here.

I wish you could stay, Ash. I'll ring you as soon as I get home, okay?

What will your mother say? Maybe she won't let me talk to you? She probably thinks this is all my fault.

I'll ring you, all right?

Yes. Bye, Rosie.

See ya, Ash.

ROSIE

Asher is gone. He looked so funny in that old man's dressing gown. We held hands. He gave me a *Mad* comic. Everything feels awful and wonderful and strange all at once. I'm falling asleep.

PIP BRINGS

A bunch of white geraniums she picked on the way

A Cherry Ripe bar, legally acquired

A note from Mr Epanomitis

Purple hair

Her best grin

MALVINA AND NIGEL

He meets her at the bookshop at two o'clock. He doesn't say where he's been. She doesn't ask. The sky is full of wisps of grey cloud and the street is empty. They head towards the taxi stand but before they get there Nigel stops at an old white station wagon. Gets out a key. Gives it to her.

What's this?

What does it look like, dollbaby?

It looks like a car, but whose is it?

Yours. Mine. Ours.

Ours?

Yeah. Ours. I thought I might stick around for a while. Give it another shot.

It?

Us. That is if you want to.

Nigel, are you saying this just because of Asher?

No. I'm saying it because I missed you both like hell and I think we can make it work. I really want to try. What do you think?

I think . . . I think this is one of your better ideas.

What about Asher?

Asher?

You reckon he'll let us?

Yeah, I reckon he probably will.

✉ THE NOTE FROM MR E

It was made from purple art paper folded into a card with a hand-drawn border of daisies and peace signs. Written in black Texta it said:

GET WELL SOON, ROSIE AND ASHER!

Double English hasn't been the same without you guys. We've got Tennyson, we've got Kerouac but we ain't got you. Good wishes from all the students, and from Tim Epanomitis.

HARRY

Hi, Rosie. I bought you most of a Flake bar. It's a little squashed but it still tastes good.

Thanks, matey. How are you doing, squirt?

Don't call me that. I'm okay. I had to stay at Ned's house. I slept in the top bunk. Haven't you got a telly?

Nah, you have to hire them. You can watch the one in the day room if you want.

Where's the day room?

Down there.

Can I go and have a look, Mum?

Well, don't get lost. So how are you feeling, sweetie?

Better. I slept most of the afternoon. Pip came for a little while. Her hair's purple now. It looks ace. And Asher came to see me after lunch.

How is he?

He's okay. They discharged him. Mum, I can see him, can't I?

Well . . . yes, within reason.

Like what?

Like, let's talk about it when you get home, darling. We'll sort something out.

Mum?

What?

I'm glad I'm home.

Mum, Mum, I found the room but it's only boring old *Sesame Street*. Can I play in the lifts? Hey, Mum, why are you and Rosie crying?

Because we're happy, that's why. How about you sit on the chair and read the *Mad* magazine.

Yeah, okay, but Rosie?

What?

Can I eat your Cherry Ripe?

TWO WEEKS LATER/HARRY

Today I got into the soccer team. Practice is on Tuesday after school and we play on Saturdays at the oval. Mum is going to buy me these special shoes that cost $34. I've got black shorts already and I get given a team jumper on the day. The mothers take turns at washing them. Mum says she'd rather be a kid and get to roll in the mud.

Rosie has been home for ages now. Mum made her dye her hair back to dark brown because it was growing out. It was black at the roots and the rest was yellow. Mum said it looked tacky. For once Rosie did what Mum said. They are getting on at the moment. It can't last. Asher dyed his hair back to brown, too. They had to sit on the patio with brown goo and Glad Wrap on their head for twenty minutes. I wanted to take a photo but I wasn't allowed. Get this. Asher is Rosie's boyfriend now. He comes around to watch TV and they sit on the couch and hold hands. All this lovey-dovey stuff is spew-making. That's what Ned and I think. Beethoven is still sleeping with me. Rosie tries to sneak him away but I save little bits of my dinner like sausage or chop bone and keep them under my bed. It really works.

ASHER/FRIDAY EVENING

after school today i went to this counsellor guy mum and dad thought it would be a good idea he is a nice guy a big bloke with a beard easy to talk to a bit like leo his name is tony we talked about the accident i feel kind of guilty about dave and about all the worry we put everyone through but tony says i need to let myself off the hook he said get on with your life and enjoy it one day at a time tony asked me how my life is going i told him pretty good dad and mum getting back together again is absolutely amazing i never thought it would happen school is better than it was mrs hyde is being sugary sweet what a faker we are doing abseiling i have made two more friends thomas is brilliant man he is funny and leon is cool he comes from tasmania tony asked about rosie i just smiled didn't want to get another safe sex lecture to tell you the truth we haven't actually done it yet we muck around a lot we see each other all the time she is the nicest girl i ever met jesse sent me a card she is going out with sam the world sure is full of surprises i am saving for an electric guitar going to sell my camera and get a saturday job to score the rest of the money we are going to form a band we have lots of plans nearly time to watch the movie wonder what's in the fridge how about a plate of cold apricot crumble and a good dollop of vanilla custard life is sweet

ROSIE/SUNDAY MORNING

Yesterday was Malvina's birthday. She and Nigel and Asher and I went out to a Turkish place for dinner. We had champagne and beautiful bread and garlicky dips and souvlaki. I gave Malvina some rose-geranium bath oil wrapped in silver paper with pink raffia. Asher gave her a pair of blue bead earrings we found at the markets and Nigel bought her a book of haiku. Nigel is really great. Next week he's flying back to Byron Bay to rent out their house and then he's off to Darwin to do some job or other and then he's coming back. I was terrified they were all going to go back to Byron Bay to live but they're going to stay in Perth for at least a year, and see what happens after that. I can't believe Mal and Nigel got back together! Ash is rapt. He doesn't look sad any more. In the holidays they're going camping down south and they invited me along. Mum said she'd think about it. We've been getting on okay lately. It's not perfect but at least she is trying to let me be me. Asher comes over all the time and we're allowed to go out if I get home by eleven. I'm working on her to make it midnight. The only embarrassing thing is that Mum keeps trying to talk to me about sex and condoms. Pip keeps asking me as well, whether me and Ash are boofing. We haven't yet. Nearly. One day I would like to have a baby though. Like in about ten years. And I'll call it Lotus, or Posy. But there's absolutely heaps of things I need to do first. First we're going to get a band together. Pip can play the flute and next term she's going to learn the saxophone. Asher is saving up for a really good guitar and I'm going to do vocals. All we need is another guitar player, a drummer and maybe a keyboard. Thomas Corkingdale said we could come over to his place and jam. He has this cheapo electric guitar and his brother has an amp. We still haven't decided on what to call the band. Asher thinks The Derelicts, Pip reckons Fruitloop Highway but I think Ragged Scarecrow. We're still thinking about it. As well as the band we want to get a station wagon with a good set of tyres and a lot of grunt, and go around Australia. We'll catch up with Star and Leo, camp out in amazing places, pick fruit when we run out of money, check out the music scene in Sydney. Then maybe I'll go to uni and become a famous writer. All we have to do is finish school first. My name is Rosie Moon. My star sign is Aries. I come from a line of women who have flower names. I am nearly sixteen. I live near the sea. I like reading, roses, swimming, late nights, chocolate, clouds. I have short, curly, dark brown hair and a tiny scar where my nose-ring used to be. I'm hungry for a juicy life. I lean out my window at night and I can taste it out there, just waiting for me.